MRS. SMITH'S
SPY SCHOOL
◄FOR GIRLS►

MRS. SMITH'S SPY SCHOOL FOR GIRLS

Beth McMullen

ALADDIN

New York   London   Toronto   Sydney   New Delhi

ALADDIN

An imprint of Simon & Schuster Children's Publishing Division

1230 Avenue of the Americas, New York, New York 10020

First Aladdin hardcover edition July 2017

Text copyright © 2017 by Beth McMullen

Jacket illustration copyright © 2017 by Vivienne To

All rights reserved, including the right of reproduction in whole or in part in any form.

ALADDIN and related logo are registered trademarks of Simon & Schuster, Inc.

For information about special discounts for bulk purchases, please contact Simon & Schuster Special Sales at 1-866-506-1949 or business@simonandschuster.com.

The Simon & Schuster Speakers Bureau can bring authors to your live event. For more information or to book an event contact the Simon & Schuster Speakers Bureau at 1-866-248-3049 or visit our website at www.simonspeakers.com.

Book designed by Laura Lyn DiSiena

The text of this book was set in Chaparral Pro.

Manufactured in the United States of America 0617 FFG

10 9 8 7 6 5 4 3 2 1

Library of Congress Cataloging-in-Publication Data

Names: McMullen, Beth, 1969- author.

Title: Mrs. Smith's Spy School for Girls / by Beth McMullen.

Description: First Aladdin hardcover edition. | New York : Aladdin, 2017. |

Summary: Twelve-year-old Abigail is shocked to discover her elite boarding school is really a cover for a huge spy ring, and must undergo Spy Training 101 in order to save her mother, who happens to be the spy ring's top agent. Identifiers: LCCN 2016042030 |

ISBN 9781481490207 (hardcover) | ISBN 9781481490221 (eBook)

Subjects: | CYAC: Spies—Fiction. | Boarding schools—Fiction. | Schools—Fiction. | Adventure and adventurers—Fiction. | BISAC: JUVENILE FICTION / Action & Adventure / General. | JUVENILE FICTION / Mysteries & Detective Stories. | JUVENILE FICTION / Girls & Women.

Classification: LCC PZ7.1.M4644 Mr 2017 |

DDC [Fic]—dc23

LC record available at https://lccn.loc.gov/2016042030

For Max and Katie

MRS. SMITH'S
SPY SCHOOL
◄─ FOR GIRLS ─►

Chapter 1

NEW YORK CITY. EIGHT MONTHS AGO. WHERE THINGS TAKE A TURN FOR THE WEIRD.

Dear Abigail Hunter,

It is with great pleasure that we welcome you to the Smith School for Children's class of 2019. We are confident you will contribute many amazing things to our school and community. Here at Smith we take our motto very seriously: *Non tamen ad reddet*. Not to take, but to give back. We strive each day to make the world a better place for our fellow human beings because this is what matters most.

Attached please find details regarding the start of the school year. Our travel office will be contacting you shortly to arrange transportation for you and your belongings to our beautiful Connecticut campus. We look forward to an exciting and rewarding year!

Sincerely,

Lola Smith

Headmaster, The Smith School for Children

The Smith School for Children? What? There has to be a mistake, because I go to Sweetbriar Montessori with Rowan and Ainsley and Blake and Alec, and we have plans. Next year, in eighth grade, there's the epic three-day field trip to Washington, DC. And Blake and I trade lunch every day because he likes the kale chips and other inedible green things my mother packs for me. Speaking of my mother, "Mom! Get in here right now!" I yell.

My mother, the smart yet apparently forgetful Jennifer Hunter, appears in my bedroom doorway. She has a towel wrapped around her hair and one covering her torso. Her mouth is full of toothpaste.

"What?" she mumbles through the foam. "Are you on fire?"

I hold up the letter high so she is sure to get a good look at the Smith School crest and coat of arms, bright red and blue. (Also, why does a school for kids have a coat of arms?)

Mom squints. She's vain, so she avoids wearing her reading glasses unless the situation calls for splinter removal. I clear my throat.

"Does the Smith School for Children ring a bell?" I shout. Mom freezes, a look of shock clouding her face. Toothpaste rolls down her chin. My stomach sinks. This letter is no mistake.

"Hold on," my mother says. "I gotta spit." She turns on her heel and leaves. She could have swallowed the toothpaste, but she's angling for time. She needs a minute to determine the best way to tell me she's sending me to boarding school and just kind of forgot to mention it.

I sit cross-legged on my bed. In my free hand, I hold a ceramic box I made in pottery this year. It's glazed purple and orange and fits perfectly in my palm like a grenade. Not that I plan on throwing it or anything.

My mother returns in a white T-shirt, her long, wet hair dripping on the floor, a totally inappropriate smile plastered on her face. She eyes my pottery. The smile falters.

"Don't you even think about throwing that at me," she says, taking a seat on the end of my bed. "I'll duck, it'll smash on the wall, and what will you get?"

I put down the ceramic box. "Nothing," I mutter.

"Exactly," she says. "No upside. Just like when you ditched school with Ainsley to liberate the lemurs at the Central Park Zoo. There were police involved. No upside."

"The lemurs were not happy," I mumble. "And you're dripping all over my bed."

"I'm sorry you got the letter," she says, frowning. "But since when do you pick up the mail?"

"I was trying to be helpful," I say. "Didn't you say it would be nice if I was more helpful? Besides, it was addressed to me."

"The Smith School is the most prestigious boarding school in the country," she says.

"I don't care," I say indignantly. "I'm not going."

"You can wear skirts with little whales on them and polo shirts and things," she says. "It'll be a good fit. Lots of smart kids. Accomplished. You know."

This is a ridiculous answer, even by Mom standards. I mean, how much can any kid accomplish by age twelve? The correct answer is . . . not much.

"Are you mad?" I ask. "I've never seen this place! I've never even heard of it until right now! I go to Sweetbriar Montessori. I have friends! I have plans!"

"The Smith School is really nice," my mother offers. I

pick up the ceramic box again. She shakes her head ever-so-slightly. I put it down.

"I don't care if it's nice," I whine. "I'm not going."

"You are." Mom takes me by the shoulders and looks deep into my eyes. I hate when she does this. It's mesmerizing, like she's some kind of snake charmer, and although I've been her daughter for my whole life, I'm still powerless against it.

"You're smart, Abigail," she says. "But you need focus and discipline, and it's my responsibility to find the place where that focusing and disciplining can happen. I need you to be safe."

It's true I sometimes get into trouble. For example, two months ago I rigged the student council elections and got caught mid-ballot-box-stuffing, but that was out of loyalty to Josh, who really wanted to win and probably wasn't going to. So is loyalty bad? I think not.

The Sweetbriar principal has called me a chronic user of poor judgment. Usually he's red in the face when he's saying this, and my mother is sighing loudly in a chair in front of his desk.

"Boarding school?" I say again. For someone with a sharp tongue, I have a pathetically monosyllabic argument against boarding school. But to my credit, I'm in a state of shock, having just learned not five minutes ago that I will soon be disappeared into the green Connecticut landscape. I shake the letter at my mother.

"I will die in this prison," I say. "I will shrivel up and disappear just like the Wicked Witch of the West. My creative self will be forever silenced. I cannot possibly go."

Mom sits back and looks at me, a slight arch to one of her professionally engineered eyebrows.

"Plus, I hate polo shirts," I add. "When have you ever seen me wear a polo shirt? And what sort of person wears marine life on her skirts? Wicked Witch of the West, Mom. Poof! Gone in a puff of smoke. The end of Abigail Hunter as you know her."

"Steam," Mom says.

"What?"

"The Wicked Witch didn't burn. She steamed."

Whatever. I hug my knees to my chest, the defensive posture of a hedgehog under attack. Mom looks me up and down.

"Listen," she says with a sigh. "This is going to be a complicated year. There are places I have to be and things that . . . need doing. I can't be watching over you every second, pulling you back from the edge, intervening every time you take a wrong step. It just won't work. Smith will challenge you and keep you focused. Give it a try. Please? For me?"

Mom has the most amazing violet eyes, and right now they tell me I ought to give in. This is the closest she will ever come to begging, and it doesn't happen very often.

I love my mother. She's fun and funny and treats me with respect even when I mess up, which is frequently. But she also failed to mention she was sending me to boarding school in September. So I wait to see what else she's going to put on the table.

Mom stands up. She paces the short length of my narrow bedroom, thinking.

"Okay, how about winter break in Switzerland?" she says. "We can ski or build snowmen or, I don't know, drink hot chocolate."

I shake my head. I hate the snow. Besides, Mom drives on icy roads the same way she drives on not-icy roads: fast and terrifying.

"Tahiti?" she offers. "St. Barts? Galapagos? The Costa Rican cloud forest?"

Now she's talking. "I'll take Galapagos and that art history camp in Rome you said I was too young for."

She eyes me. My heart races. The elusive victory is close, I can feel it. Mom puts her hands on her hips. A trickle of sweat runs down my back.

"Done," she says finally. We shake hands. And while I'm ecstatically happy (I won!), I also know I've been had. Because just like that, I'm off to the Smith School for Children.

Chapter 2

THE SMITH SCHOOL FOR CHILDREN. NOW. WHERE I'M ABOUT TO MESS UP BIG-TIME.

SHE IS NOT MRS. SMITH.

I know this because if I stand at one end of Main Hall and shout her name, there is a lengthy pause before she responds, as if she's thinking about who this Mrs. Smith person actually is before realizing, *Oh right, that's me—I'd better turn around.* And if you throw out a *Hey, Mrs. Stein!* or *Mrs. James!* or any old random name, she does the same thing. A pause, a slow pirouette, and a smile so icy I can almost see my breath. Plus, if she's really Mrs. Smith, where is Mr. Smith? Why have we never seen him? Or even heard him mentioned in polite conversation? What did she do with him? All of which raises the question, who is this lady in charge of the Smith School?

Of course, we have theories, me and my best friends Charlotte Cavendish and Izumi Sato. But we lack evidence, which is why at two a.m., rather than sleeping snugly, I'm dangling out the window of my first-floor McKinsey House dorm room on a sheet tied to the leg of my desk. My best friends lean out and watch.

"Are you down yet?" Charlotte whispers. But really it's more of a yell.

"Be quiet!" I yell back.

"You two are hopeless," Izumi groans. I'd argue but I'm clinging to a sheet in the middle of the night, still a few too many feet from solid ground for comfort. I ease down slowly until my feet hit the earth. I exhale sharply. My shoulder muscles burn.

"She made it!" More yelling from Charlotte. She'd make a terrible ninja. I give my friends a thumbs-up and they high-five. Now for the fun part.

I experience a thrill as I slip into the Smith School Main Hall through a side door I left wedged open earlier. I can't believe it actually worked! I'm pretty good at this espionage stuff.

Once inside, I pick up the trail of Mrs. Smith, or whoever she is. She's headed down Main Hall to her office at the north end of the building. My bare feet are silent on the polished wood floor, and if I stay in the shadows, I'm sure she won't see me. Besides, my black Batman pajamas render me practically invisible. Better than invisible. I'm unexpected.

Mrs. Smith pulls a key from around her neck and unlocks her massive office suite door. She is never without the key. If you misbehave and wind up standing before her desk, she will hit you with that icy smile, twirling the key in her fingers all the while. Are you in trouble? Does she even know you're there? After a moment or two, her gaze will fix upon you and you'll confess to crimes you didn't even commit.

Mrs. Smith glides inside to the secretary's area, leaving the door ajar. She then proceeds to the inner sanctum with a heavy wooden door all its own, which, naturally, begins to close behind her. No! Don't close! No, no, no! I can't very well dive for the door without giving myself away, so instead I squeeze my eyes shut and will the door to stay open. It does, but just barely.

However, "just barely" works for me. I ease forward into the empty secretary's chamber and pause for a moment to see if I'm noticed. Nope. I slip by the desk and flatten myself against the dark paneling, just to the left of the inner door.

Through the two-inch gap, I see Mrs. Smith standing in front of her desk, looking at a person seated in one of the two exceptionally deep and fluffy chairs facing her desk. I cannot see who it is, but she wrinkles her nose as if her guest smells bad.

"We've talked about you making an appointment," she says coldly. "This two a.m. business is growing old."

"Considering the circumstances," comes a man's voice, "I'd think you'd be happy to get my advice whatever the time." The voice is low and menacing, but from this position I can't see the source.

"Excuse me," Mrs. Smith says in a tone reserved for turning mere mortals to quivering jelly, "but I don't need your help."

"Are you sure about that?" Mystery Man replies.

There's a lot of tension in that room. I need a better view. Who's in the chair? Who dragged Mrs. Smith out of bed at two a.m.? He doesn't sound familiar. I want to see his face. I wedge a toe in the just barely open office door and give it a shove. It's a massive slab, eight inches thick at least, and my slight shove creates enough momentum to swing the door wide so it crashes into the interior wall.

This was definitely not part of my plan.

I leap out of view as Mrs. Smith reels around.

"What was that?" Mystery Man asks. Mrs. Smith strides toward the door. She's going to slam it shut and my herculean efforts will have been for naught! I will not slip into her office undetected. I will not dive under the big brown leather sofa and quietly listen as she confesses all I need to know. I will not return to McKinsey House a hero. Except that . . .

. . . the phone rings, the big old one on her desk with the curly cord and all the buttons. And she clearly doesn't want to miss this call because she forgets all about the door and practically throws herself at the phone.

I'm so lucky. I might be the luckiest Batman-pajama-wearing, stealthy ninja girl on the planet! Before I lose my nerve, I get down low and army-crawl into the office. I keep the big brown leather sofa between her and me. I'm as silent as . . . well, I'm really quiet, anyway, and neither Mrs. Smith nor Mystery Man seems any the wiser.

Now all I have to do is listen as Mrs. Smith reveals what happened to Veronica Brooks, a senior with white-blond hair and a mean lacrosse game who seems to have vanished into thin air. My friends and I agree that if anyone knows the truth, it's Mrs. Smith, and spying on her might help us uncover it. Of course, I volunteered. It didn't seem so different from that time in Morocco when I snuck out of my room at midnight, through the fancy hotel gardens, and into the bar to free the caged parrots hanging in the corner. (Although on that night my mother caught me. Tonight is going better already!)

Hidden behind the sofa, still flat on my belly, I take a chance and peer around the edge. I can see Mrs. Smith from my position on the floor but only parts of the man. In one hand, he holds a piece of paper with a frayed edge. It's creased and folded, like someone was practicing origami but couldn't commit. I can also see his feet, clad in boat shoes and no socks despite the freezing February temperatures. The rest of him is swallowed up by the enormous chair.

But despite my good luck so far, Mrs. Smith does not reveal all. Instead, she murmurs into the phone while Mystery Man grows increasingly impatient. He taps a pencil on the arm of the chair in a frantic staccato until it flies out of his hand and lands mere inches from my face. I hold my breath. If he reaches for it, we will be nose to nose. But Mystery Man hails from the lazy school of picking things up. He reaches out a boat shoe and slides the pencil back toward him. As he does, his pant leg rides up and I get a glimpse of something colorful on his pale white calf:

a triangle-shaped bruise maybe? Hard to tell in the low light. Mrs. Smith murmurs for a bit more before replacing the receiver and returning her attention to the man.

"Can we get back to this now?" he asks, waving the paper around. Doesn't he know who he's dealing with here? Mrs. Smith doesn't appreciate emotions like impatience. Actually, she has little tolerance for the display of any emotions. This guy is clearly an idiot. She snatches the paper from his hands.

"I don't know what it is," she hisses. "I've said that already. Several times."

"Here we are, on the verge of finally determining the Ghost's identity, and suddenly, for the first time, you can't decipher the clue? Is that a coincidence?"

"Are you accusing me of something?"

"Should I be?"

"How dare you," she says. "I've given my life to this job and you know it."

"You were best friends!" the man shouts. "You're supposed to know what the clues mean. That's how this works."

"That was a long time ago," Mrs. Smith says quietly. "Things change."

"You do understand that if this evidence falls into the wrong hands, your career is over?"

Mrs. Smith sighs. "We don't even know what she found, if anything. You're jumping to conclusions."

"The government people believe it," Mystery Man says. "They're breathing down my neck. They want results. They want the Ghost."

I have no idea what they're talking about, but I try and memorize the exact words anyway so I can report back to the girls later. Mrs. Smith takes a deep breath. She balls her hands into tight fists. I wonder for a second if she plans on punching this guy in the face. That would be a story. I'd be famous just for telling it!

"Listen to me, old friend," she fumes. "I haven't worked with Teflon in a decade. We don't even trade holiday cards. To expect me to be able to get inside her head after all that time and figure out what she's doing is insane."

Teflon? A code name? The intrigue deepens. The girls are going to love this.

"So we're going to lose this opportunity to get the Ghost because you two had a disagreement ten bloody years ago?"

"Enough!" Mrs. Smith shouts, making me flinch. "I run things now, not you. And I don't like the idea of using the girl on some wild-goose chase. It's dangerous!"

"Teflon is deep under and no one knows where the

evidence is except for her. So unless you can figure out the clue she left you, I don't see that you have a choice about using the girl. Get a line on Teflon and send her out. I won't have everything fall apart because of your incompetence."

Mrs. Smith levels a menacing gaze in his direction. He's gone too far.

"Get out of my office," she growls. "Now. And next time, make an appointment."

There's a pause. I barely breathe.

"You'd better find a way out of this mess," he says. "Your superiors are not going to be as kind as I am."

I'm so focused on this heated exchange that for a moment I don't notice an image now projected on the wall to the right of where Mrs. Smith stands. It plays like a movie, in soft focus, at first blurry, but becoming quickly sharp. A cold sweat breaks out across my forehead. I jam my fist in my mouth. It can't be. But it is, clear as day. A girl. With white-blond hair. She's bound at the wrists to a chair. Two tiny holes in her neck, vampire-style, gush blood stark crimson against her pale skin. A deep scar along her chin pulses angrily. Her blue eyes look right at me, which, of course, is impossible.

"Help me," she whispers. Do I actually hear her or am I reading her lips? "Help me. Please. Oh, I need help. Yes, I do."

And then Veronica Brooks leans her head back and laughs as if this is all just the funniest thing in the world. There's something about the laugh that's familiar, but I don't have time to process it because now blood runs down her face and into her mouth. Her skin transforms into something scaly and rank. She keeps laughing, a hyena mad with the kill. When the laughing finally stops, she's facing me again, but it's no longer Veronica. It's something hateful and terrifying, with black empty eyes and a voice scraped raw as if by broken glass.

"I see you, Abigail Hunter," it says, lips pulled back over rotting teeth. "You'd better get out of here fast. Before you get caught!"

And that's all it takes to make Batman-pajama-wearing, stealthy-ninja-girl me faint dead away.

Chapter 3

WHERE I DEMONSTRATE A HIGH LEVEL OF STUPIDITY FOR SOMEONE WHO IS SUPPOSED TO BE SMART.

WHEN I OPEN MY EYES, I imagine I'm back in my tidy shoe-box bedroom in New York. But then I see Nurse Willow, an elderly gray-haired lady with deep wrinkles around her eyes and mouth. Nurse Willow would never be in my shoe box at home.

"How are we doing, dear?" she asks. Her voice is sweet, like warm honey, and I let it wash over me. The infirmary sheets are clean and smell of springtime. I nestle down a little deeper. I will simply go back to the nice dream I was having about Quinn Gardener begging me to be his girlfriend. Nurse Willow takes my hand.

"Now, now, dear, time to wake up," she coos. "Mrs. Smith would like a word."

Mrs. Smith! I give an involuntarily yelp. Quinn goes right out the window.

"Not to worry," Nurse Willow says. "I don't think she'll be too tough on you. Although there will be consequences."

Listen, Nurse Willow, you live here in the cozy bubble of your infirmary. You have no idea how tough it is out there for an invisible Lower Middle. Back at my old school I was never afraid of the principal. Actually, I felt kind of sorry for him. He was always mopping his sweaty forehead with a hanky and shrieking. But Mrs. Smith is something else entirely. She never raises her voice. She never has to. Her mere presence is terrifying enough.

Maybe she'll kick me out. Okay, that's a potential upside I didn't consider. Sure, my mother will kill me, but she can't really kill me, right? I don't have a chance to enjoy the idea of expulsion because suddenly Mrs. Smith looms large, a perfect contrast to Nurse Willow.

Mrs. Smith is petite and lean, with thick blond curls and blue eyes that give away nothing. No one knows how old she is. Forty? Fifty? A century-old vampire? She wears a preppy khaki-colored suit and four-inch stilettos. A

Smith School lapel pin winks at me from her jacket. She peers down over tortoiseshell glasses.

"Miss Hunter," she says. Her voice is smooth and deep. "How do you feel this morning?"

In a perfect world, I'd have a snappy comeback to explain my presence behind her office couch at two a.m. Something about sleepwalking or having zombie apocalypse nightmares—anything to make me appear the sad little boarding-school waif rather than the girl breaking and entering. But for all my apparent smarts, I'm tongue-tied.

"Um. Well. I. Ah. Gee. Um."

"Well then," she says. "Let's ask another question, shall we? What might you have heard during your clandestine nighttime trip to my office?" She's perched delicately on the edge of my infirmary bed, like a butterfly on a narrow stem. "What do you remember?"

Remember? An image of the Veronica creature rises up before me. I gulp and gesture for the water glass. Mrs. Smith hands it over without ever taking her eyes from mine. I'm being interrogated. It's not as bad as Chinese History with Mr. Chin or live electrical wires, but I sweat anyway.

"It's okay," she says. "You can tell the truth."

I sip my water and decide to go for pathetic. "I couldn't

sleep and I saw your light on and I thought maybe we could, I don't know, talk about how much I miss my mother," I say. "But I tripped and fell. I must have hit my head. And I definitely didn't hear anything."

The incredible lameness of this response registers in Mrs. Smith's eyes because the truth is that Batman-pajama-wearing, stealthy-ninja-girl me took one look at a bloody Veronica and fainted dead away. How completely mortifying.

Her fingers wrap around my wrist and squeeze, ever-so-gently. "Tell me what you heard, Abigail."

The sweat runs freely down my back. "I swear I didn't hear anything!" I blurt. "I snuck into your office on a dare and tripped over the carpet!" When in doubt, double down on the lame excuses.

She releases my wrist. "It's okay," she says. "Relax. I understand." Which is not the same as believing, let me tell you. She leans in close and pats me on the head like a dog. I can smell her perfume, a light floral scent much too fun for her.

I shrink down into my blanket. Mrs. Smith stands, smoothing the invisible wrinkles out of her suit pants. She's in the doorway when she says, "One more thing."

"Yes?" I pull the blanket up to my nose.

"How did you get out of the locked and alarmed dormitory?" she asks.

Oh, this one is easy. This one I can answer. I'm even a little proud, which I should immediately recognize as the beginning of my downfall. But sadly, I don't, and I give her the details.

"Sheets," I say. "Tied together and roped around the leg of my desk. I wedged the desk under the window so it wouldn't slide. No big deal. Plus, I'm only, like, one story up."

An arctic wind blows in on Mrs. Smith's smile.

"Not anymore," she says.

Chapter 4

McKINSEY HOUSE DORMITORY. FOURTH FLOOR. YES. FOURTH FLOOR.

THE SMITH SCHOOL IS A preppy ground zero of ivy-smothered buildings, rolling green fields, well-manicured gardens, inspirational fountains, and orderly stone walls. Except in February, when it resembles an ice cube.

At Smith, we have our own way of doing things. For example, seniors are seniors, juniors are juniors, and sophomores are sophomores. Makes perfect sense, right? Yes, but after that the whole thing goes off the rails. The ninth graders are Upper Middles, the eighth graders are Middles, and the seventh graders are Lower Middles. However, the middle of what, no one will say.

But us seventh graders do know that regardless of what

they call us, our true status is *invisible*. We learned quickly that if we want to survive the jungle that is the Smith School's social hierarchy, we'd better own that invisibility and make ourselves scarce. There is no lower life-form in the universe than a Smith School Lower Middle. I mean, even cockroaches can pull off the neat trick of living for a few months without a head, which is better than what we've got.

The McKinsey House fourth floor has many names, among them the Arctic, Siberia, the Sahara, and the moon. The reason for this is the rooms haven't been renovated since 1812, the showers never have hot water, and the pipes rattle and hiss so loudly at night you'd swear you were under attack by a pack of angry snakes. The fourth floor is punishment. It's where dreams go to die. Yesterday I lived on the first floor. Now I live up here. That'll teach me to pull a Batman out my window.

Charlotte lies on my bed, Izumi sits on my dresser. When you're at boarding school, you spend day and night with your friends, so it pays to choose wisely. We liked one another instantly, although physically we're an odd three-some. I'm tall and skinny with dark eyes and hair that refuses any attempt to subdue it. No matter the season, my skin color is a deep tan that—if you look at my mom—

clearly must have come from my father. Not that she's say-ing either way.

By contrast, Charlotte walked right out of the J.Crew catalog with the came-over-on-the-Mayflower family pedigree to match. Her family name is on one of the giant office buildings in New York City that I used to pass on my way to school. I've seen her smile and pout her way into privileges the likes of which the rest of us humans never even dream.

Izumi is short and sturdy, or that's the way adults describe her. She calls herself a tank, but proudly. She plays a mean rugby game and takes calculus with the seniors. Plus her mother is the ambassador to Japan and her father is some sort of venture capital genius who, according to the Internet, has more money than God.

It's evening study hall, and we're supposed to be doing homework. We're not.

"Nice room," Charlotte says, gesturing to my new accommodations and making a face.

"This is what happens when you jump out your win-dow," Izumi points out.

"I didn't jump," I grumble. "I lowered myself. On sheets. For you guys."

"You volunteered," Charlotte reminds me.

Charlotte was the first person I met at Smith on drop-off day for new students as I lugged boxes to my room. She was lying in the dormitory's wide front hallway with a copy of *Anna Karenina* on her face. Just beyond her was another girl, also on the floor, but this girl was twisted up like a Cirque du Soleil performer having a bad day. As I tried to step around Charlotte, she reached out and grabbed my ankle.

"Don't," she whispered.

"Huh?"

"That's Veronica. Don't disturb her while she's in twisted lizard pose. It's really hard. And then she'll be mean to you. But she'll probably be mean to you anyway."

I squatted down on the floor next to Charlotte. "I once saw a girl wrap both legs around her neck and walk on her hands," I whispered.

"Yoga?" Charlotte asked.

"Nah," I said. "Khao San Road in Bangkok."

"You've been to Bangkok?"

"I've been lots of places," I said, rolling my eyes. I didn't know it at the time, but my passport full of stamps from exotic locations would be my ticket to street credibility with the girls. They had private-school pedigrees and rich, important parents, but I'd been to Timbuktu. Literally.

"I have a better view from up here," I tell my friends, as if exile to Siberia is no big deal.

"Of what?" Izumi asks.

Nothing! "The lacrosse field," I say.

She eyes me. "You're acting weird."

"I was trapped in the infirmary with Nurse Willow and Mrs. Smith for at least ten minutes."

"I can't believe she didn't expel you on the spot."

"I know." Despite the room change, I feel as though I got away with something. But the other shoe has to drop. This is Mrs. Smith we're talking about. Charlotte rolls toward me.

"Can we cut to the chase, please?" she begs.

Right. A full reporting of my ill-fated attempt to infiltrate Mrs. Smith's office in the dead of last night is required. I gave the McKinsey girls a few bits and pieces over lunch, but they want the full story. They have waited all day for this moment, whereas I've been mostly dreading it.

"So I go out the window," I say.

"Yes," Izumi says impatiently. "We know that part. The sheets. Now you live on the moon."

"With an awesome view," I point out.

"Keep going."

"I make it across the quad . . ."

"No dogs?"

"I timed it so Betty and Barney were on the other side of the building." Betty and Barney are the giant Dobermans that patrol the grounds of the Smith School for Children at night. Some dogs are cute and lovable. Betty and Barney are not those dogs.

"Wow," Charlotte says. "You're good."

"I cross the quad. I enter Main Building."

"Locked?"

"Nope. Wide open."

"That's convenient."

"I could have picked the lock. Jennifer taught me how."

Here at Smith we refer to our parents by their first names, as if they're somehow our equals. Or maybe we're just superangry with them for abandoning us and it's petty revenge. I even address my mother as Jennifer on the phone now. She sighs but has yet to demand I stop, which just means she's still guilty about the whole boarding-school thing and I have to continue taking advantage of the situation while I can.

"Jennifer's cool," Charlotte says. I'm always surprised that Charlotte with her Mayflower pedigree and Izumi with her ambassador mom and megarich dad find my single, unemployed mother cool.

"She's okay, I guess," I say with a shrug. "Anyway, I creep along Main Hall." I spring out of my desk chair to properly reenact my escapades, although my very tiny new room makes this a bit of a challenge. "I hear Mrs. Smith in her office. I don't think that woman ever sleeps. Anyway, she's in there talking to some guy. He was giving her kind of a hard time. Kind of yelling."

Charlotte sits up. "He was yelling at Mrs. Smith?"

"I know," I say. "Shocking."

"Terrifying! Who would do that? Who would be brave enough?" She shudders at the thought. "Did you see him? Who was he? So then what happened?"

Well, then I saw the bloody Veronica projected on the wall and it said I should run and I fainted, if you want the truth. But I can't tell the girls this. You simply cannot say you're seeing monsters and expect to maintain any sort of credibility. I'd be done for. Everyone would know that Abigail Hunter couldn't handle the pressure and lost her marbles. So I do what any girl in my position would do. I lie.

"And then I tripped and fell," I say. Fortunately for me, they take it and run.

"And you hit your head," Charlotte says.

Yup.

"And got busted," Izumi adds.

Yup again.

"And landed in the infirmary."

Indeed.

"But did you learn anything about Veronica?" Charlotte asks impatiently.

Well, let's review what we already know about Veronica. First, she's a senior and beautiful in an ice-princess sort of way, her only flaw being a scar along the left side of her chin. And, of course, Veronica's smart. Not only does she take all AP classes, she's the captain of the debate team, and they're nationally ranked. But that's not enough. She's also the captain of the soccer team, the ice hockey team, and the lacrosse team. To make her even more annoying, she's a monitor. This means she lives in McKinsey House (in a room that's bigger than my apartment in New York, I might point out) with us invisibles. As a monitor, she is meant to gently guide us with her years of wisdom and experience. When we have problems, Veronica is where we go. Except we don't because she's so mean even the mean girls are afraid of her.

I offer the following example to illustrate Veronica's character so you don't think I'm exaggerating. Every morning we have a mandatory school meeting, which I don't believe has ever been canceled in the history of humankind. During the school meeting, students sit in assigned seats in Main Auditorium. Veronica and I both have aisle seats, although she's at the back of the auditorium and I'm in the front. It was the first week of school and an unfortunately dorky girl named Doreen made her way up the aisle. Veronica saw her coming and stuck her foot out, fast as lightning, tripping Doreen. Doreen went down hard, glasses flying, uniform askew, sprawling awkwardly on the ground. As a few students rushed to help her, Veronica looked me dead in the eye. And she smiled, as if saying, *See what I can do if I want to?*

Of course, I wanted to curl into a ball and disappear, but I couldn't break eye contact. It's as though she'd cast a spell over me. Not that I'm suggesting she's a vampire or anything, because I don't believe in that nonsense and you shouldn't either. But still, Veronica is something to see. If you could, which you can't, because she's vanished without a trace.

Anyway, the word on the street, or, in our case, the manicured pathways crisscrossing the campus, is this: Veronica Brooks was here on Monday afternoon. On Monday night, there was loud screaming heard from one of the empty Main Hall classrooms. Fire trucks and ambulances roared through the Main Gate, screeching to a halt along the large circular driveway. People came in and people went out.

And then, with the last sliver of moon casting eerie shadows on the buildings, the trucks and the ambulances drove off into the night. The kids in Main Dorm, perched on top of Main Hall, stared out their windows like the little girls from *Madeline* looking for their dog. Of course, we didn't hear or see a thing from McKinsey House, but why would the Main Dorm kids lie?

At Tuesday's school meeting, Veronica's assigned seat was empty, but no one in authority saw fit to mention it or the sirens and the flashing lights from the night before. Instead, things went along as if all was normal. The head of the English department announced a fiction contest open to all upper-school students. The dean of students reiterated that the catacombs were strictly off-limits. The Madrigals said they were auditioning new singers Wednesday after classes in the Black Box Theater. And the captain of the boys' basketball team reminded us to come out and watch the game on Saturday against archrival the Meadows School, after which we all shuffled off to class, crafting and launching at least two hundred rumors about the mysterious disappearance of Veronica Brooks along the way.

A small sampling of those rumors: She was abducted by aliens. She was bitten by a vampire. She became a zombie. She got the plague. She drank Coke and ate Mentos and exploded. She told Mrs. Cartwright, head of student affairs, to go bite it. She hit someone. She stole the bronze bust of Channing Smith, the Smith School founder, from the lobby. And, finally, my personal favorite, she dropped dead from the cafeteria food.

So really we know nothing about Veronica.

Chapter 5

THE ANNEX. WHERE TOBY STEALS THE FRENCH FRIES AND THE OTHER SHOE DROPS.

WHEN THE STUDY HALL BELL RINGS, we head to the Annex, the small, grungy snack bar where all Smith students congregate for the hour between evening study hall and lights-out. Seniors and juniors get the nice chairs and couches at the front of the Annex, while the rest of us fight it out for the uncomfortable wooden booths in the dark corners, where the smell of greasy food and old socks clings like fog.

We manage a booth in the back facing the entrance, a tray laden with cheese fries, Cokes, and Snickers bars on the table before us. We haven't planned to meet Quinn and Toby, both Middles, but it doesn't matter. Sure enough, five minutes later, Toby and Quinn enter and make a beeline for our table.

Quinn Gardener is a boy who can actually get away wearing pants with little whales on them without looking like a dork. Tall and lanky with a sweep of shaggy dark hair hanging in his face, he listens to retro eighties music like the band Talking Heads and wears docksiders with no socks. Plus, he hails from the preppy hamlet of Greenwich, Connecticut, and is a double legacy here at Smith, which means his mother and his grandfather both attended the school. With a pedigree like that, he would have to pee on the big ugly portrait of Channing Smith in Main Hall to get expelled.

Unfortunately for my dizzy brain, he can't keep his eyes off Charlotte, and I'm not a huge fan of rejection, so I keep my dizziness to myself. The boys slide into the booth, and Toby immediately dives into the fries.

"Hey," I say.

"What?" Toby gives me a well-practiced look of innocence.

"Charlotte, you look nice," Quinn says. "That's a great color on you."

"Ugh," Izumi says.

"Exactly," Charlotte agrees. She doesn't return Quinn's affections. She says she can't like a boy in whale pants. She likes Xavier, who's an Upper Middle and doesn't know she's alive. Xavier doesn't wear whale pants.

"Buy your own fries," I say, slapping Toby's hand.

"Grouch."

"Jerk."

"Can you two shut up?" Izumi asks politely.

"Did you do something different to your hair?" Quinn asks Charlotte. I swear you can almost see the little stars and hearts twirling around Quinn's lovesick head. Charlotte rolls her eyes. I eat fries.

"Did you guys hear Ceci Lyons got busted in the catacombs last night?" Toby throws out. Toby Caine, usually found floating somewhere in Quinn's wake, has chocolate-colored skin and brown eyes and dresses in a calculated disheveled way meant to imply he doesn't really care about any of Smith's nonsense. He's never without his leather jacket. The story goes that his father, Drexel Caine, scientist, collector of weird things, owner of DrexCon, the most popular video game developer in the world, and Smith School board of trustees member, flat-out forgot Toby's twelfth birthday. The very expensive jacket showed up six days later from some store in London, with no apology. Toby makes sure we know he wears the jacket ironically, and that is all he is willing to say about his father.

More important, Toby seems to know things no one else does. And for us, these tidbits are catnip. We lean forward.

"Ceci Lyons the junior?" I ask.

"Yup." Ceci Lyons is one of Veronica's friends. These mean girls are dropping like flies.

"No way," I say.

"Yes way," Toby says.

"How?" Charlotte asks. Toby shrugs. If he knows details, he's not sharing.

"And?" Izumi prompts.

"She's gone," Toby whispers, eyes bright.

"Wow, that was fast," says Quinn.

The very first thing we, the student body of Smith, were told at our very first school meeting was *Don't go down in the catacombs*. Naturally, I had no idea what this meant. Catacombs? Where are we anyway? Ancient Rome? I think not. I've been to Rome, and the people there don't wear whale pants.

Eventually, I discovered that the catacombs are actually a maze of subterranean, spider-infested, mostly uninhabitable space that run beneath the older buildings of the school. But I get that "catacombs" sounds way better than "scary basement."

If you're caught in the catacombs, the penalty is

immediate expulsion. Which means tomorrow at school meeting we will again be reminded not to go down there because bad things happen when you do. Ceci Lyons's head on the proverbial spike.

We're having a moment of silence for Ceci Lyons when my smartphone pings. All our phones are laid out on the table, as if we're playing a round of smartphone blackjack. Smartphones or any device more technologically advanced than pen and paper are prohibited during school hours, which is the reason we clutch them like life jackets on the *Titanic* from the minute classes end until we go to bed. Even though it's obviously mine beeping, everyone simultaneously lunges for their phones in the hopes that the text is for them. But really, almost everyone we communicate with is crammed into the smelly Annex with us.

"Not me," says Charlotte, tossing her phone back on the table.

"Me either," Quinn says. "I like your phone case, Char."

"Ugh," Charlotte says.

"Not me," adds Izumi.

"It's me," I say, pulling up the text. And this is what it says.

Disciplinary action for the following transgressions, including but not limited to: unauthorized absence from dormitory, presence in Main Hall after hours, eavesdropping, breaking and

entering the headmaster's office, violating the Student Respon-
sibility Code as it is defined in the Smith Student Handbook,
provided to each student at the beginning of term.

"What's wrong with you, Abby?" Izumi asks. "You just turned a totally weird color."

"Yeah," says Charlotte. "Like, green."

Slowly, I turn my screen to face them. "The other shoe just dropped," I moan. My friends pass around my phone, shaking their heads in sympathy.

"Your mom's going to go ballistic," Charlotte kindly points out.

"So what's the actual punishment?" Quinn asks. "It lists the crimes but not the consequences." As if on cue, the phone pings again with another message.

Pursuant to section 11A in the Student Handbook, you will: serve sixty hours on work crew to include kitchen duty, bathroom cleaning, and tutoring Tucker Harrington III in Chinese History three times weekly until such time that he passes the final exam. Any grievances may be lodged with Mrs. Smith directly.

There's silence at the table. Quinn lets go a long low whistle. "Wow, that Tucker thing is just cruel."

Charlotte regards me with pity. "Yeah," she says. "This might be worse than being expelled. At least with expulsion you can experience your humiliation in private. Tucker Harrington? Really? You should complain."

"Are you kidding me?" Toby says. "It could've been worse."

"How?" we ask in unison. Tucker Harrington has an IQ of twelve and a mean streak a mile wide. He's only here because his grandfather built the ice hockey rink.

"Well . . ." Toby shrugs. "I don't actually know."

"Maybe I should have told her the truth," I mutter. "The hitting-my-head story was not my best work."

Charlotte zeros in on me. "What did you say?"

Oops. "Nothing?"

"You clearly said something about the hitting-your-head story not being any good," she says. "Which is the story you told us."

"Yeah," says Quinn, because he will take every chance to side with Charlotte. Toby looks utterly disinterested in this conversation. Instead, he licks the salt off his fingers one by one. Funny, because he never misses an opportunity to skewer me.

"So what really happened?" Izumi demands.

This is an all-around terrible evening. First Tucker and now this? Okay, so I lied. I'd rather be set on fire than admit this while sitting across from Quinn Gardener, but alas, I have no choice.

"All right. Maybe the thing in the office didn't go down exactly like I said it did." Charlotte raises her right eyebrow almost to her hairline. Izumi gives me the skunk eye. The boys pick bits of cheese from the cafeteria tray and ignore us. They don't find the missing Veronica and our attempts to uncover the truth fascinating in the least. I launch into a retelling of my break-in. When I come to the Veronica-slash-passing-out bit, Toby laughs as if I've just said something hilarious. The laugh reminds me of something that feels important, but before I can place it, Charlotte leans across the table and punches Toby.

"What was that for?" he asks.

"You're a jerk," she says.

"Me? What about her?" He jabs a finger into my bicep. I shove him away.

Before we can start an all-out war in the booth, the bell rings, indicating it's time to return to our respective dorms. As we make our way back to McKinsey, we pass Tucker Harrington and his posse of morons.

"Hey, freaks!" Tucker yells with an evil grin. "Watch this!" He then shoves a passing Lower Middle into the partially frozen Smith School Cavanaugh Family Meditative Pond and Fountain.

That's it. I am so out of here.

Chapter 6

ESCAPE FROM PRISON. I MEAN THE SMITH SCHOOL FOR CHILDREN.

JUDGING BY RECENT EVENTS, two a.m. is generally an hour when things go poorly for me. But I sling my backpack over my shoulders and cinch the straps snug anyway.

"Are you sure running away is the best idea?" Charlotte asks me again.

"You could talk to Mrs. Smith," Izumi suggests.

"Tucker Harrington the Third?" I say.

"I see how Tucker might seem like an insurmountable obstacle," she says. "Where will you go? Paris? Milan? Barcelona? Is there anywhere you haven't been already?"

"I have, like, ten bucks to my name," I point out. "I'm

going home to beg Jennifer to let me drop out. I figure with the Tucker thing, she might let me."

Charlotte double-checks my getaway supplies.

"Money?"

"Yes."

"Phone?"

"Yes."

"Flashlight?"

"Yes."

"Passport?"

I roll my eyes.

"You never know," she says, wagging a finger at me.

I leave out the window. It seems Mrs. Smith overlooked the fact that a girl can just as easily tie four sheets together as she can two. Of course, the probability of falling to my death increases exponentially with each sheet, but I choose not to think about that. I take a deep breath, grab hold, and start to shimmy down. My friends lean out the window and watch.

"Good luck!" Charlotte yells.

"Thank you."

"Don't fall," Izumi says.

"I won't."

"Concentrate!"

"Stop talking to me!"

"Call us from the bottom."

"No."

"Text us, then. This is freaking me out."

"How do you think *I* feel?"

"Text us from the bottom."

"Fine!"

"Shut up!" Charlotte yells. "Stop yelling! You wanna get caught?"

By this point, I'm practically at the bottom, but I text anyway because I said I would. On the ground, I veer toward the senior girls' dorm and, beyond that, the country road that lies on the other side of the tidy stone wall. It's freezing out here. February is not the ideal month during which to run away from boarding school. As I pass the dormitory and traverse the small frozen brook behind it, I swear I hear footsteps a beat behind mine, like a fast returning echo. But when I peer over my shoulder, there's nothing. I write it off as a product of my pounding heart and sweaty palms. I don't even want to think about what Mrs. Smith will do if she finds me out here. She will have me scrubbing toilets by day and tutoring the whole demented ice hockey team at night for the rest of my life.

I push this thought away and instead concentrate on how to get to New York City from the Smith School. I don't have much money, and if I was going to call for a ride, I should have done it before I left school. There's no cell service once you leave campus. There's nothing but cows, and I can't exactly go back now. At least I Googled the nearest bus stop before setting out, but that doesn't make the two-mile trudge any more fun. Some people like the country. Usually, those people have driver's licenses.

I finally arrive to find a concrete bench next to a sign indicating this is, in fact, the bus stop. I sit in the dark and focus on not freezing to death. I work on the speech I'll give Jennifer when I show up at our apartment for breakfast. I'm sure when I explain about Tucker Harrington she'll take pity and let me stay.

By three thirty a.m., I'm on the bus to Stamford, Connecticut. From Stamford, I'll hop a commuter train to Grand Central Terminal, followed by the subway downtown, landing me at home with seventy-five cents to spare.

I lean my head against the bus window, suddenly tired. After a full day of classes, I had mandatory volleyball practice today for almost two hours. Everyone has to play a sport at Smith because it builds character. They tell us it's important to be a team player. Honestly, I don't see how getting all sweaty while frantically lurching around for some stupid ball makes me a better person.

As sleepiness creeps in, a man takes the empty seat beside me. He wears a dirty tweed overcoat and a dark wool watch cap. Sweat dots his nose and upper lip, which makes me wonder why he doesn't shed the hat or the coat. He smells musty, like he's been sleeping in a hay bale.

As my seatmate crosses his arms against his chest, I catch a glimpse of a tattoo on his forearm. It's a thick triangle with each segment a different color. I've seen something like this before. I rack my brain trying to remember where; tattoos aren't allowed at Smith, so maybe back home in New York?

As I churn through possibilities, I wiggle my elbows. Logic says if I poke this guy hard enough, I'll create an awareness of his body crossing the invisible line into my personal space and he'll move. Except . . . nope. Instead, he throws me a cold curious stare and twists his extralong legs into lotus position right on the bus seat. He then props his hands into prayer pose, effectively pinning me to the window. I let loose a loud fake cough and jam my elbow deep into the guy's ribs.

"Problem?" he snaps. His frosty eyes and perfect teeth are all wrong for a coat that would work better with rotten teeth and rheumy eyes. The effect is supercreepy.

"No?" I say.

"So what, then?" He has an accent. British? Swiss? Jennifer would know. She can call an accent at fifty yards, blindfolded.

"I sneezed," I explain. "Sorry."

The man nods slightly in response. He doesn't seem surprised to find me alone on a bus in the middle of the night, a bus full of empty seats. Which makes me wonder, why is Lotus Man sitting next to me?

His manicured fingernails sparkle in the harsh fluorescent lighting as he strokes his chin. My heart speeds up. Everything about this man—his clean-shaven face, his perfect sideburns—is wrong.

"Where are you headed?" he asks. The intensity of his gaze makes me squirm. I feel examined. Stranger danger times ten. The bus pulls into the bay in front of the Stamford train station, the darkness cut just barely by weak streetlights.

"Excuse me," I say, standing. "This is my stop." I throw my backpack on and attempt to step over the contorted man to the aisle. But nighttime doesn't seem to be bringing me luck lately. The man unfurls a leg, raises it up, and blocks my way.

"Where is it?" he growls. "We know she has it. Now,

what did she do with it?" Without a second thought, I give his leg a swift kick, pushing his knee outward at an awkward angle.

"Ow!" he bellows. "You little . . ."

I jump over him and land in the aisle. He grabs me around the waist with both hands. I sink my untrimmed fingernails into his flesh. He howls again, loosening his grip just enough that I can break free. I run up the aisle. The driver, wearing earbuds and singing, doesn't appear to notice the maniac chasing me.

I sprint by her and fling myself to the sidewalk. Lotus Man follows close at my heels. I dash into the Stamford train station. My backpack smashes me in the spine, but there's no time to adjust it.

Across the wide, deserted waiting area is the ladies' room, the door propped open by a yellow cleaning sign. I run for it. Lotus Man follows. Kicking the yellow sign aside, I charge into the bathroom and slam the door. There's a weak lock that won't hold my guy for long, so if I'm going to do something I'd better do it fast. I spy a small window that faces out of the station and onto the platform, where a handful of people wait for city-bound commuter trains. It'll be a tight fit, but I have no choice.

The restroom door rattles. I climb up on a sink and

throw my pack out the window. I hear an immediate thud, so I'm probably not high up enough to die when I jump out this window. Maybe just break an ankle or two. The door strains under the pressure of Lotus Man shouldering it. I wedge myself in, appearing to the outside world as if I'm being born through a tiny window.

Finally, I pop through and fall five feet flat on my face. I won't lie. It hurts. None of the waiting passengers look up, their faces bathed in the eerie light of smartphones. In the bathroom, the lock gives, and Lotus flies in. It takes him about a second to realize where I've gone. He's tall enough that he can just barely stick his head out the window.

"Get back here," he snarls. "Or you'll regret it."

I regret so many things right now I don't even know where to start. Blood runs from my nose. Lotus Man tries to push through the window. First one shoulder and a long arm, but there's no way he can fit despite his seeming ability to contort himself into a pretzel. If he wants me, he'll have to go around, and this really makes him mad.

At the same time, the bright headlights of an inbound train appear. I am lucky. I am stealthy ninja girl. And I'm totally screwed if Lotus Man gets out here in the next sixty seconds. His eyes register everything I'm thinking except probably the ninja bit. He pulls his arm back in the window and disappears.

The train slides into the station with a whoosh of exhaust, and the doors open. The passengers file on.

"Four forty-two express to Grand Central Terminal! No stops. Four forty-two, express only! Please have your tickets ready!"

I wedge myself into the pack and board the train. The digital sign indicating the track number and train's destination reads 4:41. One minute.

I see Lotus barrel around the corner, coattails flying. He's lost the watch cap, revealing a head of thick white hair. It's 4:42.

"Come on," I mutter. "Close doors. Close!" The train is crowded. A number of commuters in tidy gray suits and shiny shoes are staring at me now. I wipe the blood from my nose on the back of my sleeve and shrug. No one asks if I'm okay. A bell sounds. The doors begin to slide shut. Yes!

But then, from my position near the doors, I see just the back of Lotus Man's coat as he jumps on the train one car down. Pulling my backpack off, I heave it between the closing doors. A buzzer goes off. I pull the doors open another inch and wedge my body into the tight space between them. A final shove and I fall back out on the platform. The train speeds away, taking my backpack with it. Lotus Man meets my gaze with a look of pure fury as his car passes. I'm about to be happy, being alive and having escaped and all, when a hand wraps around my mouth and everything goes black.

Chapter 7

WHAT YOU THINK YOU KNOW? WELL. YOU DON'T ACTUALLY KNOW ANYTHING.

I'M FLAT ON MY BACK. At first I think I'm still in the infirmary, having a series of bizarre, head-injury-related nightmares. But it doesn't smell like the infirmary and I'm pretty sure I'm lying on concrete staring up at a white ceiling. I try to roll over, but a burst of pain runs from the top of my head all the way down to my toes. I groan. I blink my eyes a few times, willing them to focus. Everything wears a hazy halo. My head aches as if I got hit with a baseball bat at the base of my neck. Did I? I attempt to roll over again with the same results.

"Don't move," a voice says. In a flash, I remember

escaping from Lotus Man. How could he have gotten me? He was on the train! I saw him! Unless he had a partner? I never considered that. I bring my hands to my temples and push in, hoping to relieve the pressure.

"If you move," the voice comes again, "you'll just make it worse." Worse how? For my head? For my chances of survival? Now is not the time for an economy of words. I finally make it to my hands and knees, but lifting my head proves impossible. I think I might puke.

There are feet before me. Shoes. Girl shoes. Stiletto heels, in fact, attached to feet attached to legs attached to someone very familiar. I'm having a serious nightmare. Yup. That's the only explanation. And my nightmare stars Mrs. Smith, who, in my hazy state, looks like an angel, which is weird, all things considered.

She lifts my chin so we can see each other better. Another wave of nausea threatens to overwhelm me. It's as if I just got off the Tilt-A-Whirl at a carnival, and I've never been a big fan of the twirly rides.

"Abigail," she says. "You're safe. You fainted and hit your head." I have got to stop doing that. "Try and focus. You're fine." A glass of water appears in my field of vision. I roll back on my heels and take it. My hand shakes and the water sloshes all over my pants. I gag on the first sip. The second is easier. I chug the glass, wiping my mouth on the back of my sleeve when I'm through.

"Where am I?" I ask, my voice rough.

"You're fine," she says again. That's not what I asked, but before I can repeat my question, another figure appears beside her. The missing Veronica Brooks.

"You're alive!" I yelp before I can stop myself. Veronica levels a heart-stopping glare at me. I sink back toward the ground. "But I saw you in Mrs. Smith's office and you were a mess and you had vampire bites or something and you told me to run and . . ." I trail off when I realize I sound ridiculous.

"For the record," Veronica says to Mrs. Smith, "I'm totally sick of this."

"I know," Mrs. Smith sighs. "But it's necessary. You know that. We aren't just about ourselves but rather the greater good. Yes?"

"I guess," she says. But she doesn't sound convinced.

"Can someone tell me what I'm doing here?" I ask quietly. "Or, you know, where 'here' actually is." My head pounds. I'd like nothing more than to go back to my bed and lie down for eight or nine years. Mrs. Smith and Veronica each take an arm and pull me to my feet. This is bad for my head. It swims in the haze and my body goes limp. But they don't let me fall.

They deposit me in an awkward heap on a beige suede couch. I do the blinking thing again, trying to clear my vision. Slowly the room comes into focus. It's window-less, with a low ceiling, and painted entirely white. The lights are so bright you could do surgery in here, although I hope that's not on today's agenda. Next to the couch are a couple of chairs and a coffee table, a cozy living room dropped into the command center of some futuristic mili-tary police force. A rectangular steel table sits in the cen-ter of the room surrounded by eight white leather chairs. A variety of unidentifiable gadgets litter the table. Nine large flat-screen monitors are mounted on the wall to form a rectangle. On the opposite wall are about fifteen round clocks, all labeled with international destinations. At the far end of the room is a door. And standing beside that door is Toby, staring at his shoes and shifting his body weight side to side.

I'm having a very strange day.

Mrs. Smith sits down beside me on the couch. "You'd probably like an explanation," she says.

"Yes, please," I say. But instead of offering said explana-tion, she turns to Veronica.

"Can you bring Abigail something to eat?" she asks. "She looks like she needs a few calories."

Veronica makes a face like she just swallowed a bug as she disappears through the door by which Toby continues to stand and contemplate his shoelaces. I have a thought: I'm here because Toby turned me in. A flare of anger ignites in my stomach, but that doesn't make sense because Toby didn't know I was busting out of Smith unless one of the girls told him and my friends aren't traitors. So how did I get from the train platform to here? Is this the place they bring you for punishment when tutoring meatheads and cleaning toilets isn't enough?

"I'm going to tell you some things that may surprise you," Mrs. Smith begins. "This isn't the normal course of things, you understand, but circumstances being as they are, we find we have no choice."

My visual haze recedes a little, but Mrs. Smith still wears a halo. She gets up from the couch and begins to pace. She goes about as far as the steel table, spins, and comes back. Repeat. I assume the standard hedgehog defensive posture: a small tight ball.

"Can I call my mother?" I whisper.

Mrs. Smith stops pacing. She stands before me. "Abigail,"

she says. "There are times when our great nation is under a lot of stress. And when that happens, we call upon an elite force to help combat the many evils we face. Sometimes the Center is all that stands between us and chaos."

"The what?"

"The Center. Our organization." Is it me or does her tone suggest I'm a complete idiot for not already knowing that? "Do you hear what I'm saying, Abigail?"

"Yes." Which is not the same as understanding what she's saying. Veronica returns with a plate of toast that she practically throws at my head. Mrs. Smith doesn't notice because she's back to pacing.

"No one ever suspects a child," Mrs. Smith says. "Children can go practically anywhere without arousing suspicion. This is the cornerstone of our operation. We train young people to participate in the security of this great country."

The toast sticks in my throat. I must look ridiculous, gagging and choking. Mrs. Smith sighs. "Like James Bond?" she says. "Without the martinis and fast cars? Does that make sense?"

Is this what Mrs. Smith meant by "exciting year" in that welcome letter I received over the summer? "You're kidding, right?"

"Mrs. Smith never kids," says Toby. He lives! I don't know what he's doing here, but I can't believe I ever considered him a friend, even if we never actually liked each other.

"A spy school for girls," Veronica says. "You should be flattered we're even telling you about it." I feel more flattened than flattered. I shift on the couch and spill more water on my pants. Veronica looks disgusted.

"Tell us about the man who grabbed you," Toby says suddenly, stepping forward, eyes bright.

"Lotus Man?"

"Who?"

"I don't know," I say. "I just called him Lotus Man. He did this pretzel thing with his legs." I look at Mrs. Smith. "If it's a spy school for girls, what's he doing here?"

Mrs. Smith smiles in Toby's direction, a warm genuine smile that is way freakier than her usual icy one. Toby smiles back. That seals it. I'm not in Kansas anymore.

"Toby helps us with some of the technical aspects of our missions. He's the man on the ground. Or the boy."

"Him? Toby? Really?"

Her smile fades. "You sound skeptical."

Yes. But I'm not stupid. "No," I stammer. "I get it. Sure. Toby. Right."

"Lotus Man?" Toby says again. I'm scattered around like marbles on a hardwood floor. I can't keep a train of thought.

"Did he have dark hair? A scar on his cheek? Did he wear a hat? Was he armed? How old would you say he was? Did you happen to notice a triangle tattoo anywhere?"

"What? No. Yes. I don't know. He had a manicure and blue eyes and his coat smelled bad. He was skinny. He asked where it was, what she did with it, whatever that means. And yeah, he had a tattoo. How did you know?"

Toby looks ready to leap out of his skin. "That means Teflon really got what we think she did!"

But Mrs. Smith holds up her hand to silence him. "Toby, we know nothing of the sort. We only have rumor at this point and useless clues." To me she says, "Those were the man's exact words?"

"I don't know," I say. "Yes. I think so. Maybe. Is all of Smith in on this?" I don't believe any of it. It's far too ridiculous, but still. "Am I just the last to know?"

"No," Mrs. Smith says. "The school is exactly as it appears, a top-tier New England preparatory school for high-achieving students, our country's future leaders in business and public service. Very few students get recruited for purposes of intelligence gathering. And those who do are given information only on a need-to-know basis."

"Are you saying the spies don't know who the other spies are?"

Mrs. Smith narrows her gaze. My shoulders immediately tense up. "As I just said, information is on a need-to-know basis."

"And they know you do this? The people who run the school?"

"I run the school, Abigail," she hisses. "The man on the bus asked you where she hid it? He was that specific?"

"No," I say. "He didn't say anything about hiding. He asked what she did with it."

"Very interesting," murmurs Mrs. Smith. "Perhaps she really found something."

"She did!" Toby yelps. He bounces around in his scuffed tennis shoes like a live wire. And I have to ask, "What do I have to do with any of this, please?"

Toby goes back to studying his shoelaces. Veronica stands to the right of the couch, her hands folded loosely behind her back, her feet spread about a foot apart. It's an at-ease military stance that gives me a chill. A mean girl is dangerous enough. A mean spy girl sounds infinitely worse. Mrs. Smith returns to the couch. She pats my leg without warmth or affection.

"We need your help," she says. Veronica makes a face. My confusion feels like a Victorian-era corset cinched too tight, and I gulp for air. They watch me closely.

"I really want to talk to my mom," I whisper. "Can I please call Jennifer?"

"Not exactly," Toby says.

"Nope," Veronica adds.

"Actually," Mrs. Smith says, "your mother is why you're here."

Chapter 8

WHERE CONFUSION IS REPLACED BY MILD HYSTERIA.

MRS. SMITH'S WORDS HANG in the air. A very unsophisticated hiccup rises in my throat. It takes all my will to push it back down. I succeed, but now my head might explode.

"Are you okay?" Toby asks from across the room.

Am I okay? What kind of stupid question is that? Of course I'm not okay! Don't even say the word "okay" to me, okay? Jeez.

"Yes," I squeak. "Jennifer?" Mrs. Smith begins to pace again.

"Your mother is affiliated with the Center," she says, "and has been for quite a long time, in varying capacities."

The hiccup springs loose. I can't help it. Jennifer works for some mysterious spy ring? That's insane. She's my mother! She forgets to brush her teeth and where she parked the car and what time she's supposed to pick me up. She listens to music from the 1980s (and not the retro, hip kind Quinn listens to). And she never remembers to sign permission slips or homework or anything. There is just no way. I love my mom, but come on.

"No way," I say.

"Yes way," Mrs. Smith confirms.

"I don't feel well."

"You don't look well either," she says. *Gee, thanks.*

Mrs. Smith continues. "We have some questions for your mother but are having trouble locating her."

Veronica steps forward, wearing a lovely smirk. "She kind of disappeared," she explains. "Like, gone. Off the radar. Vanished without a trace. Missing in action."

"That's enough, Veronica," Mrs. Smith says curtly. "Sometimes in espionage work, the lines of communication get . . . muddled. We know that Jennifer Hunter was in New York. And then she wasn't. And it's extremely important that we speak to her. She may have something people want, and she might be in terrible danger as a result."

Terrible danger? That doesn't sound so good to me. "Did you call her?" I ask. They all stare at me. The air in the room goes thin and I squirm uncomfortably in my seat. Did I say something wrong? "Maybe she just went away on vacation? To a place with no cell service?" I know full well my mother would never do that without telling me. Since I came to Smith, she has texted me at least seven times a day to inquire as to my well-being, even if I rarely answer. But come to think of it, I haven't heard from her in the last few days. A wave of guilt washes over me. I didn't notice until now.

"No," says Mrs. Smith. "We don't think she's on vacation." Veronica smirks some more. Toby continues to avoid eye contact. "But as I said, the situation is urgent, especially in light of what happened to you last night. You're very lucky Toby alerted us to your plans. Although he was a little late in doing so."

So one of the girls did throw me under the bus! Which one was it? A burst of anger replaces my overall feelings of guilt, exhaustion, and confusion. And yes, I realize I should be grateful they saved my life, but that doesn't mean I can't be angry at the same time.

"Unfortunately, we couldn't apprehend the suspect and secure your safety, which means we were unable to question him about his role in all of this."

"It was either you or the Lotus Man," Toby adds. In the silence that follows, I wonder if they're waiting for a thank-you for choosing me over the Lotus Man. It seems a dubious honor.

"Is Jennifer going to be okay?" I whisper.

"We certainly hope so," Mrs. Smith says with an off-handedness that does not inspire confidence. I recall the day just six months ago when Jennifer dropped me off at school. She and Mrs. Smith shook hands in the formal way of two people meeting for the first time. But that can't be true, can it? If my mother is "affiliated" with the Center, whatever that means, she would know Mrs. Smith, at least from a distance. I wish I hadn't eaten that toast. It's trying really hard to crawl back up my throat.

"I'll do whatever you want me to," I say. "Whatever I need to do to help."

"We know you will, Abby," Mrs. Smith replies coolly, leading me to believe I never really had a choice. "We'll discuss the specifics of our plan later. In the meantime, Veronica and Toby will fill you in on the details of how to manage your day in light of your new . . . situation." She then sashays out the door as if we've just had a nice little chat about my F in Chinese History last semester rather than one where she revealed that everything I thought to be true actually isn't.

So here I sit with Veronica and Toby. According to the many clocks on the wall, it's six fifteen in the morning here, almost lunchtime in London and time for evening study hall in Sydney. Toby flops down on the couch. Veronica glares at me.

"I don't like you," she says flatly.

"Come on, Ronny," Toby says.

Ronny? Invisible Lower Middle Toby just called the most popular girl in school . . . Ronny? To her face?

"Give her a break." He turns to me. "Veronica's the Center's top field agent. She was on a mission when you guys thought she vanished."

"But she was all mangled," I sputter. "I saw it. The vampire bites in that video or whatever it was." The minute the words leave my lips, I know I've made a mistake. Veronica looks at me, eyes blazing.

"Did you see the actual 'vampire bites'?" She throws up her fingers in air quotes. She mimics me perfectly. She's so mean.

"No," I stammer. "I just . . ."

"Do you read all those stupid vampire books targeted at gullible kids just like you?"

"Yes, but I don't believe any of—"

She interrupts. "Sure you do. You and your friends. You sit around in the Annex and talk about the cute vampire boys, right? They're so mysterious. Blah, blah, blah."

"Well . . ."

"And who listens to you talk?"

Toby jumps in. "Ronny, don't."

"Who sits there with you? Who eats your French fries and listens to your girl gossip?"

My eyes drift to Toby, and suddenly I realize the laugh I heard in Mrs. Smith's office when I saw the Veronica creature was his.

"But I don't understand," I say.

"He did it because he could," she says coldly. "This is the kind of thing Toby does for sport." I feel oddly betrayed. Toby is back to studying his shoelaces.

"But," Veronica continues, "there's a lesson here: Don't jump to conclusions, because usually they're wrong. Got it?"

I nod. I can't look at either of them. I'm too humiliated. How could he?

"Say it," she commands.

"Don't jump to conclusions," I repeat.

"Well, aren't you so smart?" She abruptly turns her back on me as if I'm no longer there. I attempt a fetal position on the couch. "Toby, give her the lecture, will you? I can't take any more of this." She leaves, slamming the door behind her.

The room goes totally silent. Toby fidgets uncomfortably. "Listen," he says finally. "I'm sorry. I'm really sorry. I didn't mean to, you know, make you faint and stuff."

"Yes you did," I say.

"I'm sorry," he repeats.

"Whatever. What are you supposed to tell me?" I want to get this over with so I can maybe go throw up in or at least throw myself into the Cavanaugh Meditative Fountain.

Toby regroups and stands up straighter. "Okay," he says. "Pay attention. When you go back to school, act normal. Say nothing about what you've heard here today to anyone. That includes all those girls you hang around with."

Well, that's easy. Because I'm never talking to those girls again. None of this would be happening if they hadn't blabbed about my escape.

Toby glances at his watch. "It's six thirty. You can probably go back to bed for fifteen minutes if you hurry up. We'll meet again tonight to talk about the plan. Eleven o'clock. Here."

And now for the question I asked way back when I opened my eyes but nobody seemed particularly concerned with answering, which is, "And where exactly is 'here'?"

"The catacombs," Toby says. "Of course."

Chapter 9

THE CATACOMBS. WHICH AREN'T ANYTHING LIKE ANCIENT ROME.

I DO GO BACK TO BED for fifteen minutes, and I must fall asleep because I wake abruptly to Charlotte poking me in the face.

"Hey!" she yells. "Open your eyes already! What're you doing here? What happened to running away?"

"I changed my mind," I mumble.

Izumi bounces on my bed. "You what?"

"Changed my mind! I couldn't do it to Jennifer," I say. "She'd be so disappointed if I got kicked out."

"And that actually bothered you?"

"Yes!" I yell. Which one of them got me busted? They

act surprised to see me, but someone is faking. I glare at my friends. They don't notice.

"Well, you'd better get up," Charlotte says. "We're late for breakfast."

I move through my day like an ant in molasses. Every student I pass could be a spy. My head swirls with fragments of information and innuendo. What is this all about? Who are these people? Where is Jennifer? Do they have a plan? Do I get to hear it tonight? The questions pile up with no answers in sight. In Beginning Concepts in Physics, Mr. Roberts tells me I look unwell and offers to get me a cup of tea. He's a supernerd who gets totally excited when discussing gravity and Newton and stuff, but at least he's nice. And harmless. Unlike Mr. Chin. When I fall asleep at my desk in Chinese History, Mr. Chin throws me out. Mr. Roberts finds me in the hallway, looking confused, and lets me sit in his office until the next class starts. I fall asleep in his chair and drool on myself. Mr. Roberts is kind enough not to mention it. Basically, the whole day is a train wreck.

At eleven o'clock I'm once again shimmying down the side of my dorm on tied-together bedsheets in the dark because I have no idea how to get out of the locked and alarmed building otherwise and nobody offered up an alternative. I wear all black because it seems like the right thing to do.

I evade the dogs of death and enter Main Building just as I did the other night when stalking Mrs. Smith. How long ago that feels! How innocent! Boy, could we have been more wrong about Veronica or what?

When I left the catacombs with Toby this very morning, we exited via the enormous stone fireplace in Mrs. Smith's office. First, we left the shiny, white-walled rooms of the Center and entered a narrow dark hallway that looked as if it hadn't been vacuumed since the Jurassic era. Cobwebs wrapped around my face and legs as we walked, and the weird shadows thrown off by Toby's flashlight made me jump.

"Don't mind the spiders," Toby said. "They rebuild insanely fast down here. It's just something we have to live with."

I was too busy stumbling over the uneven ground and pretending he didn't exist to process the spider comment. The whole place had a terrifying carnival-fun-house vibe. I wouldn't have been at all surprised if a psychotic clown leaped out and devoured me. We snaked along for a while, passing through a set of keypad-protected doors and finally arriving at a ladder that seemed to disappear into the darkness above. Toby put the flashlight between his teeth and started climbing. The situation was so ridiculous I giggled.

"What?" he said, his head at an awkward angle so the beam of light shone right into my eyes.

"Hey," I said. "Quit that. You're blinding me."

"Sorry. What're you laughing about? Most people in your situation don't laugh." He started up again.

"Most people?" I asked.

"Usually they cry," he said. "Mrs. Smith says it's the shock. You didn't cry."

No. But I wanted to. "Is everybody in on this?"

"Mrs. Smith already answered that question," Toby said. We trudged up. How long was this ladder, anyway? Where was the elevator? Plus, Toby was not very forthcoming, and I felt he owed me for taking "jerk" to a whole new level.

Finally, we reached a submarine-style hatch. Toby bumped it with his shoulder and it creaked open. We emerged into a tiny space, barely big enough for both of us, with exposed stone walls and a sandy floor. We couldn't stand up. And we were too close, New York City subway close. My elbow nailed him in the spine, and he stepped on my foot. We muttered apologies. I started to sweat.

"Now, where's that keypad?" Toby ran his hands along

the stone walls, his flashlight beam painting loopy circles of light as he searched. "I can never find it. Ah, right. Here it is." He flipped open a panel set in the stone to reveal a keypad. Toby punched in some numbers, one of the walls began to lift into the ceiling, and beautiful, precious light poured in on us. I blinked a bunch of times. "Come on."

I followed Toby out of the tomb and into Mrs. Smith's inner sanctum. It took me a moment to realize we'd come by way of the fireplace. Quickly, Toby flipped up another panel, this one disguised as a fireplace stone, and the wall closed behind us.

"Wow," I said.

"Yeah," Toby said. "So this is the way in and out."

"What's wrong with a door?"

"Too obvious."

"Great," I said.

"Yeah."

"Do I get to know the codes?"

From his pants pocket, Toby pulled a small piece of paper covered in pencil scribbles.

"They change every month," he said, handing me the paper. "These are the current ones. Memorize. Destroy." I giggled again. Cue the *Mission: Impossible* theme.

"What?" he asks, annoyed.

"Nothing," I said. My eyes watered. "I'll eat it when I'm done."

Toby frowned. "This isn't a joke, Abby. This is about saving the world. Maybe you want to start taking it seriously."

I stared at him. Had he really just said *saving the world*?

"From what?" I demanded. "Aliens? Robots? Zombies?"

"No," he said, suddenly looking weary. "Bad people, really bad people."

If I had been less tired and hungry and angry, I maybe would have asked for an explanation, but instead I stalked off without another word.

Which I kind of regret right now. For example, I should have asked him which pencil scribble corresponds to what keypad, because if I remember correctly, there are at least five between the Center and me. Not to mention all the hidden panels.

I make my way down Main Hall, once again staying to the shadows. I have no idea how I'll explain myself if I get caught.

Oh, I'm just going down the rabbit hole to get the spy plan from the girl we all thought was dead, who just happens to hate my guts, and our terrifying headmaster so I can help find my mother and save the world, although I'm not clear exactly from what. Sure. That will work.

I arrive at Mrs. Smith's massive office door and silently push inside. The office is dark except for the glow of a desk lamp. For all the rules at Smith about cleanliness and tidiness, Mrs. Smith's desk is a mess.

Is this room monitored? Are they watching me right now? I do some jazz hands just for my own amusement. I walk around behind the massive desk. The world looks different from back here. It's like standing on the bridge of a ship. I sit in her chair. It's uncomfortable, with no cushion and a hard back. No wonder she paces.

Papers are piled high. I spot a folder with my name on it. Abigail Hunter. I have to open it. Anyone would, right? Inside I find last year's school picture and a biography of all the exciting things that have happened in my twelve years of life, like being born. I flip to the next sheet. It's my application for admission, filled out and sent off, without my permission or knowledge, by my mother. Most of it is blank, and there's no personal essay, which, according to the application, is mandatory. As folders go, this one is pretty thin. Again I wonder, *What am I doing here?* They never interviewed me and asked the all-important question that is always asked in school interviews: What dead person in history would you like to have dinner with? I'm a little disappointed to have missed out on that one because

I would have said Sherlock Holmes, although I'm not sure fictional characters count.

Next to the folder is a pencil sketch on a creased piece of paper. I recognize the rough edges of this paper. It's what the man was waving around at Mrs. Smith the other night. It's a finely detailed pencil drawing of a statue of a woman. More important, it's one of the sketches Jennifer makes when she's on the phone or daydreaming. Our refrigerator is covered with half-drawn faces and flowers and rainbows and cats with long, weird whiskers. But how did a piece of my mother's refrigerator art end up here and what did it have to do with the conversation between the man and Mrs. Smith? Before I can dig further, the fireplace rumbles and Toby emerges.

"Oh," he says, surprised. "I thought maybe you got lost or couldn't read my writing or messed up the codes or something."

I leap out from behind the desk as if I just got electrocuted. "Nope. Just, um, getting ready to go down there and get all over whatever it is we're doing down there."

"Are you okay?" he asks. "You look funny."

"I'm totally fine," I insist, charging ahead of him into the fireplace. "Let's go. I can't wait to get started!"

"Well, now I know something's wrong with you," he

says. But he follows me as I begin to descend the ladder into the darkness.

At least this time when we reach our destination, I'm on my feet rather than flat on my back. This is a plus. Not that it puts me at ease exactly. "The first time I came down here, I kind of freaked," Toby says. Yes. "Freaked" is a nice word for it.

We walk the length of the room, around the couch where I sat just this morning, and through another door I didn't even realize was there. On the other side is a smaller room with a table. Siting at the table are Mrs. Smith and Veronica.

"You made it," Mrs. Smith says, as if this were in question.

"You have cobwebs in your hair," Veronica says. She's so nice. I just bet we're going to be great friends someday. Like never.

I tell myself to shake it off. I'm here to find out what's going on with Jennifer. That's it. Nothing else matters.

Chapter 10

WHERE I'M MADE AN OFFER I CAN'T REFUSE.

MRS. SMITH STANDS UP. "Thank you for joining us," she says, as if this meeting were optional. "I thought we'd bring you up to speed on the plan, although it's still rather amorphous."

Toby messes with a laptop on the big steel table and all nine screens on the wall slide together to make one giant image of what looks like a flight itinerary. Jennifer Hunter. February 18, four days ago, which is when her daily texts to me stopped. John F. Kennedy International Airport to Charles de Gaulle in Paris. Business-class seat. Free Wi-Fi. Meal service.

"France?" I ask.

"It was about the Ghost," Veronica says.

"The Ghost?" I sound like a demented parrot.

"The Ghost is a dangerous man," Mrs. Smith says. "Wanted all over the world by everybody."

"What did he do?" I ask.

"Do?" Mrs. Smith stares at me. "'Doing' is more accurate. He ruins people." I fidget at the edge of the table. "Sit down, Abigail. You're making me nervous."

"Sorry," I mumble. I take a seat.

"Jennifer's obsessed with the Ghost," Veronica says. "Always has been."

"You might call him her nemesis," Mrs. Smith adds.

"Seriously?" I clearly didn't even know my mother well enough to know she had a nemesis.

"Yes," Mrs. Smith says.

I have a hard time imagining Jennifer hating anyone, or even being that angry. Sure, she doesn't like it when I get in trouble at school or leave wet towels on the bathroom floor or put an almost-empty milk container back in the refrigerator, but it's more annoyance than anger. What has this Ghost guy done to earn her wrath? I can imagine some very bad things.

"So why don't you guys stop him from doing whatever it is he does?" I ask.

Toby snorts. "You think it's that easy? Believe me, we've tried everything."

"But the Ghost is unique," Mrs. Smith continues. She fingers the office key around her neck. It glows in the harsh lighting.

"We don't even know what he looks like," Veronica adds. "Jennifer searched for him for, like, years until you screwed things up."

Mrs. Smith waves her off. "Veronica's sensitive," she says, as if that explains anything. "Jennifer was the Center's primary on the Ghost, but after you were born, she was asked to help with less urgent matters. A parent is inherently . . . compromised." There's an edge to her voice I've never heard before, as if she'd like to give Jennifer Hunter, once spy girl rather than spy mom, a smack in the face. "But unbeknownst to us, Jennifer continued her search. She never stopped looking for the Ghost's weakness. His soft spot. A way to bring him to his knees."

You know how when you place the last few pieces of a puzzle, suddenly the whole picture comes into focus? The little bits of blue and white are now obviously clouds and sky and the long tan streaks against a brown background are kitten whiskers. It all makes sense. I have that experience now, except it's not a puzzle, it's my life.

I have been everywhere. I have extra pages stapled into the back of my passport. I've been to places I can't pronounce. My little red wheelie suitcase is dented and cracked. I thought nothing of Jennifer rousting me in the middle of the night to catch a totally unexpected flight to, say, London. She made her living as a courier for "important things," as she described it, and being dragged halfway around the world was my ordinary. She pulled me out of bed for Marrakesh and Calgary and Tokyo and Cape Town. We went to Los Angeles and Athens and Ljubljana (that's the capital of Slovenia). And why not Stockholm, Kansas City, and Prague while we're at it?

When we arrived, there would be an appointment, some sort of meeting, always out in the open, and Jennifer would plant me on a bench or by a tree, and there I'd sit until she was done doing whatever it was she was doing. She always kept the line of sight open so I could see her, but I was never close enough to hear what was said. Typically, there were two or three minutes of conversation and sometimes an exchange of an envelope or a small package, and we'd be right back to playing tourist.

But if what Mrs. Smith says is true, this wasn't just Jennifer moving important things around the world. No, it was my mother looking for the Ghost, world-class bad guy, with me as her unwitting accomplice. What sort of mother does that?

"We know from our intelligence sources Jennifer was to meet a man named Peter Rhodes," Mrs. Smith says. A photo pops up on the screen of a man with a round bald head and beady eyes. "Peter Rhodes claimed to have information. People claim to have information all the time. This isn't unusual. Rhodes was to meet Jennifer at the Eiffel Tower."

"But within five hours," she continues, "there's this." Another picture. This time Rhodes lies on a slab, wearing a white sheet and a toe tag. Gross.

"He was found in the Seine," Toby says. "And he wasn't swimming."

"We know Jennifer came back to New York," Mrs. Smith says. "But there's been no sign of her since her return. And this is unusual."

"And you guys, you know, tried calling her and asking her and stuff?" They look at me as if I've gone completely mad.

"She wasn't supposed to be even thinking about the Ghost," Veronica says.

My mind is trying to deal with all this information so quickly that I'm surprised steam doesn't billow from my ears. "So basically you don't know where she is or what she did in Paris. And now you can't find her."

"This is Jennifer Hunter we're talking about," Toby says. "If she's gone rogue, no one will find her."

"Toby," Mrs. Smith snaps.

"Sorry," he mutters. But I heard him.

"Rogue?" I say quietly. The definition of "rogue" is one who is no longer obedient and therefore not controllable or answerable. My stomach flip-flops.

"The Center has an extensive network of worldwide contacts," Mrs. Smith says. "There's been noise on the network that Peter Rhodes gave Jennifer something important, something having to do with the Ghost. We need to know what it is. Now, there'll be a number of other parties interested in knowing this too. Unfortunately, the world is full of bad guys trying to one-up one another, so it's critically important we get to Jennifer first."

The definition of "rogue" also includes things like "renegade" and "unpredictable." A little voice in the back of my head wonders why, after years of what sounds like loyal service to the Center, Jennifer would suddenly go around them. But I know better than to ask this question. Instead, I ask how they intend to find her if she's as good at hiding as Toby implies.

"You misunderstand, Abigail," Mrs. Smith says with a jagged little smile. "We don't intend to look for her. She'll come to us."

"How?" I ask, my voice creeping up a few octaves.

"If Jennifer is deep under, she won't come up for anything except—"

"Except . . . ," Veronica says with a hint of glee.

"Except you," Mrs. Smith finishes.

"Me?"

"If Jennifer has something on the Ghost, the Ghost's going to want Jennifer," Mrs. Smith says. "Following so far?" *Kind of. Maybe.* "The Ghost's enemies, of which there are many in the criminal world, will also want Jennifer for the same reason we do. She's very popular right now. But Jennifer will only come up for you."

I begin to see where this is going. They're using me. As bait.

Toby interrupts. "So you walk around and let the bad guys come after you, and Jennifer swoops in and saves you, and we grab her and debrief." He says this as if the whole idea is incredibly fun and he just can't wait to get started. I want to punch him.

"That's the plan?" I ask. It sounds more like a hope than a plan.

"You have a better one?" snaps Mrs. Smith. She seems unusually tense, even for her. I hold up my hands in surrender.

"Okay," I say quietly. "So where do I go to be, you know, bait?" Mrs. Smith smiles and her shoulders relax just a bit.

"We're working on that," she says. "While we narrow in on Jennifer's possible location, I've asked Veronica to give you the rundown on how we do things here at the Center. We don't have much time, but used wisely, it'll be better than nothing."

This is clearly news to Veronica. "What?" she says. "Why can't Toby do it? This is so not fair."

"What's fair and what's necessary aren't always the same thing," Mrs. Smith says. "We do what needs to be done."

Veronica is obviously furious at this assignment. I hang my head. My cheeks burn. With all my heart, I wish Jennifer were here. I wish she were here so I could tell her I'm never speaking to her again for the rest of my life.

Chapter 11

SPY TRAINING WITH VERONICA: NIGHT NUMBER ONE.

WHAT ON EARTH IS VERONICA going to teach me in spy training? Kung fu? How to properly wear a disguise? How to forge a passport, an identity, a fingerprint? Will she teach me to speak fifteen different languages so I blend into local cultures like I belong? I really want to ask her who the other spies are at school, but I'm afraid she'll tell me that information is on a need-to-know basis and then karate-chop me for asking.

I follow her down a blindingly bright hallway. There are doors off the hallway on either side. We enter room number seven. Lucky seven. Or in my case, probably not-so-lucky seven.

The room is large, with a wooden floor and white padded walls that absorb the sounds of my footsteps as well as the sound of me being knocked to the ground. Because suddenly there I am, flat on my face, a victim of the same foot as Doreen way back at the beginning of the year at a school meeting. That foot is fast. That foot is an army of one. That foot is on the small of my back applying a not-insignificant amount of pressure. I groan.

"If you want to work for the Center," Veronica says, still simmering, "there are some lessons you need to learn. Lesson number one: awareness. Your environment is ever changing. If you don't pay attention, you end up on your face. Or worse."

I'm very aware that if Veronica pushes down any harder, she will rupture my spleen. I don't want to consider "worse."

"Awareness," I wheeze.

"Speak clearly, innocent!"

I can't do that because my mouth is pressed to the floor. I can barely breathe. Plus, I never asked to work for the Center! I never asked for any of this, and after only twelve seconds of Veronica training, I'm pretty sure I'm going to suck at it.

I grow light-headed from lack of oxygen. The way I see it, I have two choices. I can lie here and suffocate or I can get her off my back. I place my hands into push-up position. I have never been very strong, but I'm long, so I can create leverage. On the count of three. One. Two. Three. With all my strength, I snap my arms straight. Veronica's foot dislodges and I roll away, tucking myself into a crouch position in case she decides to kick me in the teeth as a follow-up.

"Awareness," I repeat, as clearly as I can. Veronica circles me. I remain tucked.

"Stand up," she says. I do as I'm told.

"Your job is to block. Whatever I throw at you, defend yourself."

"Wait!" I yell. "Why do I need to defend myself if I'm bait? Doesn't bait just, you know, sit there and wait for something to happen?"

Veronica takes a moment to look appalled. Clearly, I've said the wrong thing. Again. "Lesson number two," she growls. "Things don't always go as planned."

"Well, I kinda figured that one out already," I point out.

"You're hopeless," she says with an exaggerated sigh. "Sit." We both drop down on the hard wooden floor. "Listen carefully. A lot of times, bait gets eaten. Your job is to adjust on the fly."

Did she just say "eaten"?

"I have two nights to give you enough basic skills so you don't make a total mess of everything," she continues. "Not that anyone believes even I can work that kind of magic, but here we are. So I'm going to do my best and hope it's enough. It won't be, but whatever. Now get up. We have work to do."

Veronica's idea of a pep talk doesn't fill me with confidence, but I get to my feet because I don't want to find out what happens if I don't.

Turns out I should have taken my chances on the floor. Veronica's hands are as fast as that foot of hers, which I guess shouldn't be surprising. She gets me in the chest, in the neck, in the soft part of my belly. She hits my thighs, my shins, the insides of my palms. Each hit feels like a bee sting, the accumulation of which causes my eyes to water. I do my best to block her, to get my hands in place before she strikes me. But I'm too slow.

As I fail and fail again to defend myself, I think about how none of this would be happening if Jennifer had told me the truth: her job, those trips, this school, Mrs. Smith. It's a long list, and with every item I add I get a little angrier. Did she send me to boarding school because she wanted to search for the Ghost unhindered? Was I just a nuisance? She did say she wanted me to be safe, but I thought she meant from my sometimes-not-very-good choices. In any case, I'm now being beaten up by Veronica. That is definitely not in the "safe" category. I'm so mad my anger actually cancels out the sting of Veronica's lightning-fast hands.

But wait, maybe that's because Veronica isn't landing her jabs. Maybe that's because as my brain stews, my hands do the busy work of defending my body as if on autopilot. Of course, the minute I realize what's happening, the whole system collapses and Veronica gets me right in the face.

Okay. Concentrate. Think about . . . Quinn? All right, that might work. I love his hair, the way it's a little too long and curls around his ears and the blue-green of his eyes and his lopsided smile. I love how his Smith School official navy-blue blazer always looks like it spent the night thrown in a corner and his shirts are not much better. But he likes Charlotte. It's a nonstarter. WHAM! Veronica gets me in the thigh with a foot, and I stumble back against the padded wall.

Okay, Abby, time to move on from Quinn. Think about New York. Think about the courtyard pond at the Frick museum, so quiet and serene with the fountain gurgling in the middle and the lilies floating on the surface of the water. Yeah. That's good. I like MoMA, too. And Shake Shack! Oh, that's a good one. I could lose myself in fantasies about Shake Shack for days! It takes a minute to realize there's been a pause in the pummeling. Veronica, in ready position, appraises me.

"Do you want to know why I don't like you?" Veronica asks. Not really, but I bet she's going to tell me anyway. "You get special treatment because you're Jennifer Hunter's daughter."

"Huh?"

"You walk around with a sense of entitlement, like everything that was hers should be yours just because you share DNA. The rest of us work hard for what we get. We work for Mrs. Smith's respect while you just coast."

Wait a minute! Up until yesterday, I had no idea Jennifer Hunter was anything other than my mother. I'm about to say as much when Veronica's hands fly at me. But fueled by a new surge of anger, I land two sweet jabs to Veronica's sternum and push her back on her heels. It's not much, but I'll take it.

"That's better, innocent," Veronica says. She wears a funny smile. I'm in a full sweat. My body aches head to toe. I don't know how much time has passed. It could be minutes or days.

"What's with the 'innocent'?" I ask.

"It's what we call the new people," she says with a shrug. "You're all so naive when you walk in here. You think the world is safe and benign and full of happy endings and fairy dust. But you're wrong. And once you see just how wrong, all that innocence is gone. Tomorrow night, lessons three and four. Don't be late."

With that she leaves, slamming the door behind her. I guess I survived night number one of basic training.

Chapter 12

THE NEXT DAY. WHERE I'M EXTREMELY TIRED AND CRANKY.

AT TWO IN THE MORNING, I climb back into McKinsey House through Tory Agnew's open first-floor window. Why the girl sleeps with the window open in February is anybody's guess, but I'm grateful. I show my gratitude by landing with a thud, tripping over a lacrosse stick and a pair of soccer cleats, and falling headlong into the desk. An upright container of pencils tumbles over, and the pencils scatter everywhere. I catch myself on the wall and pull down an Alex Morgan poster. This is terrible. I freeze.

Fortunately, Tory sleeps like the dead. She doesn't even twitch, and I make it safely to the hallway and back up to my room. I should have asked Veronica how she gets in and out of McKinsey House, because I'm betting it's not like this. She probably has a key. Or a passcode. Or maybe she just growls at the door and it yields in fear.

Lying in the darkness, I realize it's the first time I've been alone with my thoughts since my ill-fated attempt to run away roughly thirty-six hours ago. My mind spins like an overcaffeinated hamster on his favorite wheel. My mother the wonder spy has done something she wasn't supposed to and gone off the grid. The Smith School for Children is really Mrs. Smith's Spy School for Girls. Veronica's actually more terrifying than I originally thought. And Toby, well, who is Toby? My eyes feel crusty and raw every time I blink. When I close them, bright colors flash against my lids. A flicker of pale sunlight appears in my window before I fall into a restless sleep.

The next morning, even the effort required to lift a bite of scrambled eggs to my mouth seems herculean. I push my breakfast tray out of the way and put my head down on the table.

"What's wrong with you?" asks Izumi, poking me with her fork.

"She's been like this all morning," Charlotte says. "A big drag."

"I'm tired," I moan.

My friends have very little sympathy for how exhausted I am because they don't know I spent the night being beaten up by Veronica.

"Have some tea," says Izumi. Izumi firmly believes the solution to every problem begins with tea.

"Coffee has more caffeine," offers Charlotte. Coffee is available for the upper-school students, not that we invisibles don't drink it anyway. In fact, Charlotte drinks lots of it, black, but makes awful faces while doing so.

"I hate coffee," I whine.

"Oh no," Charlotte yelps. "Here comes Quinn. Hide me."

I pick my head up to see Quinn and Toby moving toward us, Toby giving me an award-winning hairy eye-ball. How am I supposed to act normal with him looking at me like that? And how come he's so perky? He mock-toasts me with a cup of coffee. Fine. I push back from the table. "Anyone want coffee?" I ask, resigned to my fate. I cannot fall asleep in Chinese History again.

"Oh my God!" Izumi suddenly shouts, and Izumi never shouts. We follow her gaze toward the cafeteria entrance.

"Veronica," Charlotte whispers. "She's alive!"

"You have no idea," I mutter under my breath, stalking off toward the coffee urn. Veronica heads right for me. She, too, looks perky and energized. I've got to figure out how they do it, because it'll be some sort of miracle if I survive the morning, let alone the rest of the freaking day. I feel Toby's eyes on me as Veronica approaches, as if he's beaming a warning directly into my brain. *Stay cool, Abby.*

So I try. I continue to walk toward the giant coffee urn along the far side of the dining hall. Veronica passes on my left. She does not make eye contact. She does not acknowledge my existence. I'm relieved and yet oddly disappointed. I know her now. I'm one of two people in this room who know her. Or maybe there are more? How am I supposed to know? No one tells me anything. But the point is, a wink or a nod would've been appreciated, some recognition that we're in this, whatever it is, together. I'm being melodramatic, but I'm kind of cranky this morning. I don't kick her in the shins, but the thought makes me smile.

Veronica heads to the popular girls' table. They don't seem surprised to see her. I have a terrifying thought. What if all the Queen Bees are in on the spy gig, a kind of *Charlie's Angels, Mean Girls* version? I shudder at the notion. I might survive Veronica, but five or six of her? No way.

Only when I go to pour my coffee do I realize I now hold a small piece of paper. *How did she do that?* With my back to the dining tables, I smooth the paper flat in my palm.

The office. 1 hour.

I assume it means Mrs. Smith's office. In one hour, I'll be right in the middle of Chinese History. Oh, why does it have to be Chinese History? Why can't it be Beginning Concepts in Physics with Mr. Roberts? Mr. Chin doesn't even like us breathing in class, let alone up and leaving halfway through. Plus, he's already mad at me about the falling-asleep thing. I stuff the note in my pocket and head back to the table, my coffee sloshing all over as I go.

Exactly sixty minutes later, I raise my hand. Mr. Chin peers at me over his half-moon glasses. He does not like being interrupted.

"Why, Miss Hunter." He glowers. "You must be awake if your hand is raised. How lovely for us. Do you have a question?"

"May I be excused to use the restroom?" I say.

"The restroom?"

"Yes. It's kind of an emergency." Snickers from my classmates. My face flushes bright red.

"Is this a real emergency, Miss Hunter, or an excuse to sneak out of class and text smiley faces to your friends?"

"Um, my phone is in my room, sir," I say quietly. "No electronics during class time."

"It's nice to see you understand the rules," he says, "even if you feel they don't apply to you. Perhaps you intend to nap like you did yesterday?"

"No, sir," I mutter, "I just need to use the restroom." This is awful. I wonder what would happen if I crawled under my desk and pretended to be invisible? The minute hand on the clock lurches forward. Now I'm in trouble and going to be late.

"Do you think the rulers of the Ming Dynasty care that you have to go to the bathroom?"

"No, sir."

"I'll tell you what," Mr. Chin says. "Give me the year in which the Ming Dynasty began and you can go."

All eyes are on me. Do I know the answer to this question? Why, yes I do. I spent an afternoon in the Hong Kong Museum of History, and while Jennifer whispered with some guy, I learned a whole lot about China.

"The year 1368," I say. "It ended in 1644."

Mr. Chin peers down at me. I sense we're not quite done. "Who was on the English throne in 1644?" he asks.

"King Charles the First," I say. "House of Stuart." I've also been to the Museum of London.

"Very well, Miss Hunter. You may go."

I dash out the door before he can change his mind and start grilling me on which dynasty followed the Ming. I think it's the Qing, but I could be wrong.

Main Hall is the original Smith School building, constructed in 1890, when the school was founded. It has high ceilings and old lead-paned windows, and my footsteps echo as I speed toward Mrs. Smith's office.

I knock softly, still unsure if this is where I'm supposed to be. Maybe the "office" is down in the catacombs? I'm about to retreat when the door swings open. I step inside. The air in here is thin, as if I've gone up ten thousand feet just by crossing the threshold. I gulp a few times.

"Abigail," Mrs. Smith says with a tight smile. "What excellent timing. Mr. Roberts was just leaving."

From one of the plush chairs facing her desk, Mr. Roberts rises, and for a flash I swear his face is scrunched up in fury. But just as quickly, it passes and he gives me a wink.

"Miss Hunter," he says. "Feeling better?"

"Yes, sir," I say. He pats me on the head as he walks by.

"Remember," he says, "without sleep we can all go a little insane."

"Mr. Roberts!" Mrs. Smith barks.

He turns on her and grins. "Have a lovely day, Headmaster." Does he slam the door as he leaves? Did I walk in on a fight? I can't imagine being mad at Mr. Roberts. He's kind of like a giant teddy bear that is always offering tea and sensible advice. Before I can decide what's really going on here, Mrs. Smith points to one of the fluffy chairs. It's so deep I sink in to the point where my feet don't touch the ground. I swing them gently.

"You'll be flying to San Francisco tomorrow," Mrs. Smith says without preamble.

"What?" Maybe Mr. Roberts is right and my lack of sleep has made me crazy, because I think she just said I'm going to California.

"We have it on good authority that Jennifer arrived at San Francisco International sometime in the last two days."

"Why'd she go to California?" I ask.

"She's confusing her pursuers," Mrs. Smith says. "It's protocol. And no one is more confusing than Jennifer Hunter." There's that tone again, angry and annoyed. Toby said they were partners and that they stopped being partners after I was born. Maybe that didn't go over well with Mrs. Smith.

"Great," I say. "Confusion is great."

"You'll follow her out there," Mrs. Smith says. "We stick to the bait plan. Bronwyn will meet you in San Francisco. She's one of our affiliates and will be your contact." Bronwyn is the preppiest name in the universe. I had never even heard it until I came to Smith. Now I know like seven of them.

"How will I know who Bronwyn is?" I ask.

Mrs. Smith passes a photograph over the desk. It's a girl, definitely older, although I'm terrible at guessing ages, with dark hair and eyes. I can't tell because the photograph isn't that great. Her face is angled away from the camera, and her long hair creates a shiny veil halfway to her waist. It's enviable hair.

"Bronwyn will wear a black jacket with a red flower in the lapel. She'll meet you at baggage claim. The code word is 'turtle.'"

Red flower. Baggage claim. Turtle. Check.

Mrs. Smith leans back in her chair. "Understand your job here is minimal, Abigail," she says. "Do what Bronwyn tells you to do. Don't improvise. Don't make your own choices. Got it?"

"Yes," I say.

"How was your session with Veronica last night?" she asks. This feels like a trick question because I'm sure

Veronica already told her I'm a disaster. So I hedge.

"It was interesting." I did learn something, after all. I have no hope of becoming a black-belt kung fu ninja master. I've realized I don't like people hitting me. The reason I never thought about this before is because no one has ever hit me before.

Mrs. Smith appraises me as if I'm a piece of meat she's considering for dinner. "I imagine it was," she says finally. "We're done here. Toby is waiting for you down in the catacombs. He's got some items you might find useful on your trip."

"But what about Mr. Chin?" I blurt. "He probably thinks I drowned in the toilet."

"Don't worry about Mr. Chin," she says. "I'll take care of him."

This is so not a normal school in any way, shape, or form. I'm just saying.

Chapter 13

THE CATACOMBS. WHERE I AGAIN PROVE MY BRILLIANCE.

I WATCH AS MRS. SMITH flips open the rock keypad and the entire back end of the fireplace slides away, revealing the low, dark tunnel. I may never get used to this.

"I assume you remember the way?" Mrs. Smith asks, stepping aside with the gracious smile of a perfect host. I nod, hunch down, and squish myself inside.

"Don't hit your head," she says as the door closes.

Without the aid of a flashlight, I hit my head a number of times on the low ceiling. By the time I reach Toby, I'm feeling concussed. This plus all the fainting cannot be good for my health.

Toby takes one look at my red forehead and says,

"You gotta duck in the low spots, Abby." He sits at the big table in front of the wall-mounted screens, a laptop open before him.

"Easy for you to say." I take a seat next to him. "Don't you find any of this weird?"

"What?"

I gesture to our surroundings. "This!" I shout. "Everything!"

He looks. He shrugs. "No. It's not weird. If you're going to do something undercover, you need a place off the beaten path. This works well."

I sigh. "That's not what I mean."

Toby pushes his chair away from the table and pops his feet up beside his laptop. He eyeballs me. "So you really didn't know about your mother? That wasn't an act?" I refuse to dignify these questions with a response. I practice the haughty look Charlotte has down cold. "That's so totally insane," he says. "I mean, you were living with her! How could you not notice?" Clearly, I need to practice my haughty look. But now Toby's on a roll. "Dude, Jennifer Hunter was hard-core. She was amazing."

"Did you just call me 'dude'?"

"Huh?" His eyes blaze. He looks as if he might blast out of his seat on sheer enthusiasm any second now.

"Never mind," I say. "What does 'hard-core' even mean? Listen, I get she's a spy and doesn't like this Ghost guy and all, but why do you guys act so weird whenever you talk about her?"

"Before you were born, Jennifer was the best," Toby explains. "When she started here, no one knew what she'd become."

"Hey!" I jump to my feet. "Back. Up. When you say Jennifer was here, do you mean here, like Smith 'here'? The spy school for girls 'here'?"

He nods. "Yeah. Duh. She's a member of the founding class, actually."

Of course Jennifer is an alumna of the Smith School for Children. I'm an idiot who didn't see the very obvious right in front of my face.

Toby hits a few buttons on his keyboard, and suddenly a photograph pops up on the giant screen. "Check this out," he says. "The Persephone Club."

The photo is from a yearbook, a club picture with about ten girls lined up in two rows, all wearing an old version of the same horrible uniform I wear. They look happy, laughing, arms around each other. One of the girls in the front row holds a sign with the club name: Περσεφόνη. It must be Persephone in Greek, but I'm too stunned to ask, because there, right in the middle, wearing a big grin and terrible 1980s hair, is Jennifer Hunter. My mother.

I sit down hard. My vision narrows, and my scalp tingles. In the photograph, next to my mother is another girl, also with big hair and a happy smile. This is Mrs. Smith, although sometime in the last thirty years she's morphed from a smiling student to the Ice Queen. Still. Mrs. Smith and Jennifer with their arms around each other on the quad. My head is going to explode. I warn Toby to stand back and maybe cover his electronics with plastic. I take several deep breaths and sit on my hands to stop them from shaking.

As I stare at the photo, I realize it's the first one I've ever seen of Jennifer as a teenager. And until this very moment it never occurred to me why that might be. Our family photo library begins with my birth and goes forward from there. These last two days have been an exercise in humility. What sort of person isn't interested in seeing photos of her own mother when she was young?

"What?" Toby asks.

"Nothing," I say, too embarrassed to reveal my thoughts. Standing beside the girls in the photo is a middle-aged man with big, bushy hair. "Who's the guy?"

"You're not going to believe me," he says.

"Try me," I say, glaring at him.

"Mr. Roberts," he says.

"No way." Sure, Mr. Roberts is nerd cool, but not *cool* cool like this guy in the photograph, even if you account for the 1980s glasses and alarmingly plaid pants. Our Mr. Roberts is old. He's bald and wears musty sweaters with elbow patches. He can literally talk about electric current for hours. This does not compute.

"Yup," Toby says. "He was the founding director of the program. The story goes that he ran some secret operation with Jennifer and Mrs. Smith and they got the goods on this art thief that half the world was after. With that success, he was able to get money and full control. All the girls were handpicked by him. He was amazing. Mrs. Smith took over when he retired. Now he just teaches."

"He had a lot of hair," I say. "So what did Jennifer do to make her so famous?"

"All kinds of stuff," Toby says. This topic obviously thrills him. He quivers with excitement. "If there was a hot spot in the world, she was there. Russia, Syria, Pakistan, Sudan, Somalia, Bosnia, you name it."

"Good for her," I mutter. I think about the time Jennifer took me to Marrakesh. She moved through that noisy labyrinthine medina like she owned the place. I remember how dazzled I was by the colors and smells, the way the people smiled and spoke, and how little my mother seemed to register any of it. This was familiar to her and no big deal. I'm not doing a very good job keeping my hands steady.

"Jennifer was the Center's top agent," Toby says, his foot tapping hysterically on the floor.

"You talk about her like she was some kind of super-hero." I sniff.

"She was," Toby says without irony. "They called her Teflon because she could walk into the worst situation and come out clean. This country would have been completely screwed without Jennifer on the front lines. Of course, she was only half of the team. Lola, I mean Mrs. Smith, was the other. She was on the ground here when Jennifer was out in the field. They had this crazy system of transferring information that could not be compromised."

"How?"

"I have no idea," he says with a happy grin, "but they teach their tactics as standard operating procedure at the strategy school in Florida. I hope I get a chance to go when I'm done here."

There's a spy college? Do you send your transcript along with a record of how many bad guys you neutralized junior year? "So, what happened?" I ask, because the Jennifer I know and tell everything to, who obviously tells me nothing, is quite definitely not a superhero.

Toby looks suddenly wistful. "It's like Mrs. Smith said. A parent can be compromised. Everything changed after you were born."

They're going to blame me for global warming next. I just know it.

"You know, the first time I ever saw her for real was when she dropped you off." Toby leans toward me and whispers, "We were told not to ask you this, but what's she like?"

"Jennifer?" He nods, eyes bright and expectant. "I don't know." I shrug. "She's regular. She makes really good brownies, and whenever we go out, she makes me play I Spy, which is totally annoying. She's just a mom, I guess." Toby's expression indicates my answer is less than satisfying. "Well, it's not like she's constantly going around beating people up or anything. I mean, come on."

"No, you're right," he mutters. "Sorry."

My eyes drift back to the photo on-screen. I remember the stiff, formal handshake between Jennifer and Mrs. Smith. There was no trace from either woman that they knew each other and, from the looks of the photo, were actually once friends.

"Oh, shoot," Toby says, glancing at his watch. "We should hurry. I have class."

Okay, Toby. Hurry up and give me my spy gear so you don't miss Math II or whatever.

On the far wall, Toby pulls down a panel to reveal a rotating set of shelves stocked with gadgets that look ordinary but—and I'm just guessing here—probably aren't.

He pulls off an iPhone, a set of headphones, and a backpack. He places all the items gently on the table. He tells me to sit down. I do. He picks up the iPhone and admires it like he might ask it out on a date. "I love this thing," he says.

"I see that," I say.

"And I put it in an extraspecial pink leopard-skin case because, you know, you're a girl."

I want to say, *Listen up, Toby. I never liked Disney princess dresses, and I never played with dolls. I don't like makeup, and I brush my hair only because dreadlocks are expressly forbidden at Smith. So how do you think I'm going to feel about a pink leopard-skin iPhone?*

"That's nice," I say instead.

"So," he says, clearly pleased with himself, "this little guy acts exactly like a normal iPhone, but it has some extra features. It's protected by a voice recognition program, which, when I turn it on, will recognize only you." He places the phone in front of me. I pick it up and try to turn it on.

Toby screams. "Put it down! Don't aim it at anyone! Are you crazy?"

I drop the thing like a hot potato. "What's wrong with you?" I shout. "Don't give it to me if I'm not supposed to pick it up!"

"You can pick it up," Toby says, running a hand through his sweaty hair. He looks like a porcupine. On Quinn, porcupine hair looks good. Toby just looks like a mess. He slides the phone back in front of me, but I have a relatively high IQ and the basic capacity to learn, so I don't touch it. I barely look at it. "It's just really new," he explains. "And I'm not sure I've gotten all the bugs out yet."

"Great," I say. "Thanks for sharing that with me. I feel so much better."

He gently taps the screen and the Center logo appears in bright orange. He taps again and four app icons replace the logo. A gun. A spray bottle. A whistle. And an old-fashioned-looking radio. I get the feeling these aren't fun games for me to play on my five-hour flight to California. He picks up the phone and walks to the far side of the room. He turns and aims for the wall behind my head.

"First, the gun app," he says. "A high-velocity rubber bullet. It can't kill a person—you can't have real weapons until you graduate—but it can slow them down. Buy you a few seconds. Which is sometimes all the difference in the field." He taps the icon, and I hear a *ping* behind me. High-velocity indeed. I saw nothing fly by, but now there is a small hole in the wall, and on the ground at my feet rests a tiny rubber bullet. Toby smiles.

"That's so cool," he says. "Anyway, the spray bottle produces a stream of really hot water. That can also buy you a few seconds."

"Or sanitize my hands before I eat," I offer. Toby glares at me.

"The whistle's totally awesome too," he says, throwing me the headphones. "Don't use it unless you're wearing these. Okay? If you forget, it'll really suck. So the whistle emits a sound on a frequency that damages the human ear but only of someone nearby. Again, it could buy you some time."

All this talk about buying time is making me nervous.

"The radio's a direct link to us here," he says, tapping the icon. "It's always connected, no matter where you are. You could talk to me from the middle of the earth. You can see me and I can see you unless the connection is crappy.

Or the phone is dead. Then it's just a brick that I guess you could throw at someone's head if you needed to . . ."

". . . to buy some time?"

He smiles. "Yeah. But try and keep it charged."

"Okay. Got it. Can I use it to text, like, Charlotte?"

"No. It's just connected to us here."

Well, that's no fun. Toby's fingers fly over the phone. "Here," he says, "voice recognition is on. Start with the prompt 'Toby is cool' and then issue your command."

"You're kidding me."

"No. What?"

"'Toby is cool'?"

"Well, I am, and you'll realize how cool I am when you use this puppy . . ."

". . . to buy time," I finish. "I get it, I get it. So if I want to play Solitaire, I say that thing about you being cool and then 'solitaire'?"

"Yes. Except don't play Solitaire."

"Why?"

"Because for some reason the whole thing blows up when you play Solitaire." He shrugs. "It's a bug."

"You don't mean the kind of thing you can fix by turning the phone off and on again, do you?"

"No. Blows up. Boom."

I take the phone reluctantly. "Thanks," I say. "I think."

He hands me a black plastic block about three inches in length. Do spikes shoot out of it and slice up my enemy, buying me time? Or does it send a message to the aliens hovering above in their spacecraft that I'm ready to be transported off this rock? I'm almost afraid to ask. But considering some of Toby's toys blow up, I hedge my bets.

"What does this do?"

"It charges the phone," he says. "Like a battery. But way fast."

"Oh." Must get control of my imagination. Right now. He unzips the backpack.

"The pack is made of a virtually indestructible material," he says. He keeps unzipping until the whole thing is laid out flat, a giant circle of fabric. "I don't know what you want to do with it, but I think it's cool so, you know, here you go."

"Will it make me invisible?"

Toby frowns. "No." *Too bad.* He begins to zip it up. I'm not very good at puzzles, and the one time I made an origami frog it looked like roadkill, so the chances of me being able to zip this thing back up are slim. I try to pay attention, but Toby moves too fast. He plops the pack in front of me.

"Don't lose my stuff," he says.

"I won't," I promise.

"You lose things, Abby."

"I do not."

"Your backpack? At the train station?"

"That was different. That was self-defense."

"Whatever. I stuck a tracer on you at the Annex that night and you lost it. It was a good one too." So it was Toby! I level the iPhone at him, finger on the gun app. He has the decency to look concerned.

"What you're saying is none of my friends gave me up?" I ask. Toby shakes his head. "And how did you know I was going to bolt?"

He shrugs. "Tucker. Any normal person would have to consider running."

"Thanks for getting me busted." I sniff.

"I saved your life," he says, equally peeved. "I did the right thing."

"No you didn't," I snap. "I got away. Lotus Man was on the train and I was on the platform!"

"You keep telling yourself that if it makes you feel better."

"Jerk," I whisper.

"What?" he says.

"Never mind," I say. If you can't win an argument, go for mean. "So you just, like, hang out down here and tinker with electronics?" I ask. "I mean, you never go out in the field, do you? Or on missions like Veronica? You just stay home, right?"

"I don't go out in the field," he says quietly, closing up his hidden wall of gadgets. His smug expression evaporates, and I feel just the opposite of better. "I'm not allowed."

He doesn't even look at me as he leaves without another word. As I gather my gadgets into the backpack, I don't think I have ever felt as alone as I do right now. After a minute, I follow him out and make my way back to the surface.

Chapter 14

SPY TRAINING WITH VERONICA: NIGHT NUMBER TWO.

WHEN I ARRIVE AT ROOM unlucky number seven down in the catacombs, I find Veronica in a variation of the twisted lizard pose she was in the first time I saw her. But now she's so twisted it looks like her head is screwed on backward. Her eyes are closed. It's creepy.

"Hi," I say. Can she talk in this position? Is she stuck? Do I need to call for help? She doesn't answer but begins to slowly unravel. Once upright, she takes a few deep breaths.

"You're three minutes late," she says.

Well, that's because Toby finally gave me a secret override code for the McKinsey House alarm system so I could actually exit through the front door. Of course, I forgot the code and had to go out the window again. It slowed me down. "Sorry," I mumble.

"Tonight," she says, "we work on lessons three and four." I can hardly wait. Maybe those will include how to survive on no sleep or how to keep big fat secrets from my best friends? "Lesson three. Simplicity. Keep things basic. Don't get complicated. Complication leads to failure." I nod vigorously as if I have any idea what she's talking about. "An example of simple but effective is Snake in the Grass."

Huh? How did we go from simplicity to animals? Before I know it, WHAM, and I'm back to staring at the ceiling tiles. I really hate Veronica's foot.

"Stand up," she barks. I hop to my feet. "Now watch." She drops down in a squat position with her hands flat on the floor behind her. She rolls her weight onto her palms and with incredible speed shoots her right leg out in my direction. The foot of my nightmares wedges between my ankles. When she yanks her leg back, I go down in a heap. Snake in the Grass. Wow.

"I can't do that," I groan from the floor. "No way."

"Yes, you can."

"Nope."

She sighs. "We can do anything if we get out of our own way. Now you try." I don't want to. Even in practice I don't want her to take it the wrong way. "Go," she snaps.

On my first attempt I fall over backward. The second try I accidentally kick her in the shins. The third go is worse. I get my foot tangled up in her feet and then I fall over backward. It's embarrassing. On the four thousandth try, I sort of knock her over. "Simple" does not mean "easy." Veronica looks almost defeated by my ineptitude, but she takes a drink of water and regroups.

"Let's try another one," she suggests. "We won't actually do it because I don't want you to end up blind. It's called Crow." Blind? Crow? My head spins. "Come on now, Abby. Keep up!" Veronica stands with her feet wide. Her right elbow is up by her ear. She faces the padded wall and lets the elbow come down like a hammer. *Thunk!* She does it again a few times, fast as lightning. *Thunk! Thunk! Thunk!* "Ideally, you want that elbow in your victim's eye socket," she says. "But if you're too short to reach the head, any soft place on the body will do. It packs some power. Just remember a crow pecking his dinner."

I'm a little grossed out by the eye-socket thing, but I do better with Crow. After thirty minutes I'm quite confident I can defeat a padded wall. We sit on the floor and drink water. My muscles ache. "Have you ever used these on a real person?" I ask quietly.

"Yes," Veronica says. I want details. I want to know what it felt like, what she was thinking at the time. Was she scared? Did she panic? But from the look on her face I can tell no details will be forthcoming. Veronica dismisses me. "I'm going to bed," she says. "You should do the same."

I follow her out of the training room and past the couch and the steel table and the clocks. She moves fast through the dark catacomb tunnels. She can probably do this with her eyes closed. Only when I can no longer see the glow of her flashlight beam do I realize she never gave me lesson number four.

"Wait!" I yell, my voice bouncing off the tunnel's stone walls. "What's the last lesson?"

Her light moves back toward me, and when she appears, she looks ghostly, like the Veronica creature I saw projected on the wall of Mrs. Smith's office. I take an involuntary step back and hit my head.

"Ouch."

"Number four," she says. "Act normal. A normal kid is invisible to adults. At least kids like us."

And I swear she sounds sad.

Chapter 15

MRS. SMITH'S OFFICE. WHERE SHE INSTRUCTS ME ON HOW TO EXPLAIN THE UNEXPLAINABLE.

THE NEXT MORNING, I drag myself to Mrs. Smith's office for a final meeting before boarding the plane to California. I look like a zombie. I'm surprised my fellow students don't run away screaming. I'm not designed for Crows or Snakes or fleeing bad guys or buying time. I carry the pink iPhone in my pocket. It feels good there, like a security blanket but less fuzzy.

I knock on Mrs. Smith's door and she beckons me in, eyeing me skeptically. I don't blame her. No one is more skeptical about this than I am. I have a lot of questions. For example, how is Jennifer going to know I'm in San Francisco? And how am I supposed to convince my friends that I'm going to a cousin's wedding in California all of a sudden? They're pretty smart. They're going to know right off the bat that I'm full of it.

The Smith School for Children acts in loco parentis, which is Latin for "in place of parents." The adults here take on the parental role and your classmates that of siblings. It's all very cozy, but it also means it's incredibly hard to get away with lying, especially a whopper like this fake cousin's wedding. Mrs. Smith should know this. She went here, after all. She and Jennifer probably told each other everything. Bitterness rises in my throat. I get madder at Jennifer every time I think about her.

"Abigail," Mrs. Smith says. "Are you listening to me?"

No. Not even a little bit. "Of course," I say.

"You said you had questions," she says impatiently. "What are they?"

"How is Jennifer—I mean, my mother—going to know I'm in San Francisco anyway? She hasn't answered any of my texts, and when I tried calling her, the line did this weird beeping thing. And what about my friends? They've never heard of cousins in California before."

Mrs. Smith gives me a thin smile. "You honestly believed she was going to text you?" At least I can tell this is not a question that requires answering. She continues.

"As for knowing you're coming, we've put word of your travel out over our networks. Although we tried to be subtle. We don't want all the crazies in the world coming after you, now, do we?"

All the crazies? "And you think she'll know I'm coming?" I ask.

Mrs. Smith narrows her gaze. "Do you think a mother like Jennifer Hunter is not keyed into your whereabouts every second of the day? She knows what you have for breakfast. She knows if you even think about cutting class. She knows you have a crush on Quinn Gardener."

Wait, what? This is insane! I open my mouth to say so, but no sound comes out. I flap my lips like a suffocating goldfish.

"Some parents helicopter," says Mrs. Smith with a pinched expression. "Jennifer takes it to a whole new level. You just can't tell. She knows you're coming. Trust me."

"Won't she be suspicious?"

"I imagine she will be. Yes."

"And?"

"That's not our problem. We need to lure her out, and this is how we'll do it."

I don't like the sound of this, not one bit, but before I can protest, Mrs. Smith moves on. "As for lying to your friends, that's easy. You lie to one another all the time. Didn't you tell them something about tripping on a carpet?"

"But that was different," I protest. I did that because I was embarrassed by the truth. Then I got caught and ended up having to share the humiliating details anyway. In front of Quinn. This is not something I want to repeat.

"Was it?" Mrs. Smith says.

"Yes," I say stubbornly.

"It'll get easier with practice," she says, a bit nicer. But I don't want it to get easier. I don't want to do it at all. I'm uncomfortable enough with the spy school secret. But Mrs. Smith is not the kind of person who you have a heart-to-heart with about your guilty conscience. I stare at my shoes.

"Do we need to run through your travel details again?" she asks, moving on.

"No."

"Do you have any other questions?"

"Do you mean in general or about this trip?"

"What do you think, Abigail?"

"No," I mumble. "No more questions."

"Okay, good. Now tell me what you're going to do when you arrive in San Francisco."

"Meet Bronwyn. Get further instructions. Proceed as directed."

"And?" Mrs. Smith prompts.

"Check in at the scheduled intervals."

"And?"

"Don't lose Toby's toys."

Mrs. Smith rolls her eyes. She really does! "Don't worry about Toby's toys too much. What else?"

"Be careful? Pay attention? Don't talk to strangers? Don't eat too much red meat?"

"No freelancing," she says sternly.

"No freelancing," I repeat.

"And I suggest you get some sleep on the flight. You're going to have a long day." This is the first thing she's said that I wholeheartedly endorse. As I leave, she throws a "Good luck" at my back. I don't turn around. Mentally, I'm already preparing for how to lie to the girls.

As I pass the Cavanaugh Meditative Fountain, I bump into Mr. Roberts. Literally. "Sorry!"

"Oh, it's fine," he says, steadying me. "Are you quite all right, Abigail? You look pale."

I'm suddenly overwhelmed by the urge to tell Mr. Roberts everything that's going on and beg for guidance. I'm confused and worried and unsure, and none of these are familiar emotions.

"I'm fine," I say. "I have to go to San Francisco to a wedding. I'm just a little distracted."

Mr. Roberts smiles. "San Francisco, you say?"

I nod. "Yeah."

"It's nice out there. I'm sure you will have a good time. Try the sourdough bread. It's delicious."

"Yeah. See you, Mr. Roberts." *I have to go lie to my friends,* I add silently.

Charlotte is in the dorm lounge, lying on the floor, with a huge biology textbook covering her face like a tent. Izumi is sleeping on the sofa.

"Hi," I say.

"Abby," Charlotte says from beneath her book. "Did you know the appendix is pointless? It just sits there at the end of the intestine and does nothing?"

"Yes," I say. "Useless. Kind of like Tucker."

"I guess I never thought about it."

"Unless it ruptures, most people don't spend much time thinking about their appendix," I say, collapsing into a chair. The iPhone tumbles from my pocket onto the floor. In a flash, Izumi, clearly not asleep, has it in her hand. "This is cool," she says, examining it. "But it's weird-looking."

I freeze. *Please don't push any buttons,* I mentally plead.

What if there are other glitches Toby just kind of forgot to mention? I do not want to accidentally blow up the McKinsey House common room.

Charlotte removes the textbook from her face. "What are you guys talking about?"

"Abby has a new phone." Izumi waves it in the air.

This is bad. The thought of one of us losing an eye or our dorm going up in flames is becoming more and more of a real possibility.

"Where'd you get it?" Charlotte asks, leaning in for a better look.

"Um, my mom gave it to me?" Izumi ignores my outstretched hand, which is a good thing because it shakes. She's peeling off the pink case. She wants a look at the guts. If I freak out, they will know something is up.

And I want to tell them. The words bunch up in my throat, desperate to spill out. But I made a promise.

"Hey, you guys!" I yell suddenly. "What to hear something crazy?" My friends jump at my outburst, and when they do, I snatch the phone back and slide it into my pocket.

"Jeez, Abby, we're right here," Charlotte complains.

"Sorry, but check this out. I have to go to California this afternoon." I could be subtle or I could sugarcoat it as fabulous or I could manipulate the information in some clever way to make it easier for them to digest. Instead, I drop it like a bomb and wait to see what happens. And this is what happens.

"Like the state?" Izumi asks. She sits up on the couch and eyes me with suspicion. "Why?"

"Jennifer's cousin is getting married," I say. "And Jennifer's been on this big family kick lately and decided I just had to go. So off I go, I guess."

Charlotte cocks her head. "Weird."

"Totally," Izumi says.

"Very spontaneous," Charlotte says.

"Jennifer does this kind of thing," I say.

"I guess you did say that," she agrees.

"It's cool," Izumi says. "Anything's cooler than here."

"Exactly!" I exclaim.

"LA?"

"San Francisco."

"Even better," Izumi says. "So foggy and atmospheric. It's like a noir movie set all the time out there."

I wish she hadn't said that. I don't want to be in a noir movie because the girls always end up dead in those movies. I'd prefer a Disney identity-mix-up kind of thing where it turns out everyone thinks this is my life but really it's not. A girl can dream.

"Do you want to borrow my blue dress?" Charlotte asks. "It'll totally work for you." I stare at her blankly.

"That would be great," I say finally. Can it really be this easy? I'm almost home free. I've almost got this done! Charlotte puts the biology book back on her face. But Izumi eyeballs me.

"What?" I ask.

"I was just thinking," she says.

"About?"

"Well, the timing of this wedding is pretty bad." I start to sweat. Izumi is the smartest person in our grade, possibly in the world. She sees right through me, I just know she does.

"Why?" I ask quietly. My shoulders tense.

"You're going to miss the Chinese History exam," she says. "Mr. Chin is going to kill you."

I hadn't thought about that. Schoolwork seems the least of my problems. But still, it is a problem. "I'm sure he'll let me take the exam when I get back," I say with much more confidence than I feel.

Izumi narrows her gaze. "If you say so."

But now that I think about it, what do I know?

Chapter 16

THE PRICE OF SAVING THE WORLD.

MRS. SMITH IS IN AN important meeting and unavailable, so I find Toby in the library and drag him outside to the Cavanaugh Family Meditative Pond and Fountain. I pick the fountain because it makes loud gurgling noises that will mess up any attempts to record our conversation. Then I make fun of myself for being paranoid, but I don't change the location.

"What's going on?" he asks, looking aggravated. "Aren't you supposed to be leaving for the airport?"

"I have twenty minutes," I say. "So do we get academic compensation for Center work?"

"I have no idea what that means," he says.

"I have a Chinese History exam tomorrow," I hiss. "And I'm going to be sitting around being bait in San Francisco."

"Since when do you care about failing exams, Abby?" he asks. He's not being sarcastic but rather asking a sincere question. I've never been overly concerned about grades. I always figure they will work themselves out somehow. So why am I suddenly panicking over this missed exam?

"Why did you really drag me out here?" he asks.

Because I have no idea what's going on and I'm a little scared. I decide to tell him the first part but keep the scared bit to myself. I cross my arms and plant my feet the way Veronica does. "I need information."

"Well, Mr. Chin will give you an F. What can I say? He's naturally grouchy."

"I don't care about the test!" I shout-whisper.

"You just asked about it!" Toby shouts back, annoyed. "What am I doing out here, then?"

"The Ghost," I say. "You guys are all so freaked out. Now, I don't know if you're always like this or what, but just tell me, how can one bad guy be so important?"

"It's hard to explain," he says. "He's been around a long time, but things really started to get out of control when Mrs. Smith took over the school."

"You know how Mr. Roberts always asks for real-world

examples when we try to explain our answers in physics?"

"Yeah."

"Well, how about you try that for the Ghost? Tell me what he does."

"Okay," Toby says. "Let's see. How about you think of a giant wheel where each spoke is a different criminal element, like drugs and weapons and human trafficking and cyberterrorism and regular terrorism and all that other stuff you see on TV. There's even a spoke for people who sell kids. And the Ghost is at the center of the wheel. He's the guy who keeps the thing rolling. He connects everyone and helps them get what they need to commit their crimes. And they pay the Ghost for the privilege. Do you remember at the very first school meeting Mrs. Smith talked about how we all had such potential and her job was to help us reach it?"

I don't because I was too busy panicking over where I was supposed to sit, but I nod anyway.

"Well, everything the Ghost does takes advantage of the people no one is looking out for. These people will never reach their potential because the Ghost is in the way. He uses people and throws them away. Or worse. So every monkey wrench we throw into that wheel kind of feels like a step toward saving the world."

My whole body tingles. *Now, that's a pep talk!*

"And Abby?"

"Yes?" I whisper.

"Your car's waiting. Don't want to miss that flight."

He's right. I'm a monkey wrench in the spokes of the Ghost's evil wheel, and I have a world to save.

As I board the plane, I look for spies. Who here is watching me? By the time I take my seat, I'm convinced everyone is watching me. This is not healthy. I settle in and try to sleep because I'm afraid if I don't I'll be mistaken for a zombie and quarantined in San Francisco. I close my eyes and relax my shoulders. I count sheep. I count backward. I replay Toby's words in my head over and over. Nothing works. Finally, I give up and pull out the turbo iPhone. Toby says I can use the communication network on the plane even though the flight attendants say I can't.

"We don't subscribe to their regulations," he said. Whatever that means.

"Toby is cool," I whisper into the phone. "Show me the Center apps." The bright orange Center logo appears. I tap it and up pop the symbols for the gun, the spray bottle, the whistle, and the old-fashioned radio. I tap the radio and additional options appear. Chat. Text. Video. Panic button.

Panic button? He never told me anything about a panic button. I wonder if I can video the guy snoring next to me directly into Toby's brain? I seem to be striking out when it comes to seatmates lately. I pull up the text option, thinking I'll ask Toby if he happened to hide any movies on this phone, but as I begin to enter his name, a drop-down list of contacts pops up that wasn't there before. And these aren't names like Jane and John and Paul and Aunt Rose. No way. These are names like Polar North and Jericho and Bright Star. Code names. My mouth goes a little dry, but maybe that's because they deprive you of oxygen in airplanes.

What did Toby say they used to call Jennifer?

Teflon. And there it is, neatly tucked into the list between Sunburst and Unity. I click it and it jumps automatically into the To: box. I stare at the screen. Nothing pops up telling me to stop, so I type, *Hi, Mom.* Really. That's it. What else am I supposed to say? *Thanks for telling me you're a freaking spy*? An angry knot fills my otherwise empty stomach. She's my mother! She has no business going off and getting into a heap of trouble until I go to college! Plus, she's been lying to me for my entire life. Okay. Maybe not actively lying but certainly leaving out important details, and really, what's the difference? I clench my fists and fight back tears.

Veronica's number one lesson was awareness. Now, I don't necessarily trust Veronica, because she doesn't like me and probably doesn't have my best interests at heart. But maybe an awareness of what it's like to be Jennifer might help? I loosen my death grip on the iPhone and try to put myself in my mother's shoes. What would happen if there was something I'd been after my whole life and suddenly I had a chance at it? How far would I be willing to go to achieve my goal? If Jennifer has the Ghost in her sights, is there anything she won't do to get him?

Mrs. Smith thinks if I'm in harm's way, Jennifer's priority will be protecting me. I'll walk around San Francisco with a target tattooed on my forehead and let the bad guys take aim, meanwhile waiting for my mother to ride in and save the day.

But what if she doesn't? What if taking down the Ghost is more important than saving me? What if I'm Jennifer's price for saving the world?

I hit send on the phone. My words whirl away into cyberspace. I wait patiently for the inevitable error message. But it doesn't come.

Chapter 17

WHERE I LOOK FOR THE RED FLOWER.

I'M STARING OUT THE WINDOW at what the pilot says is Indiana when the iPhone vibrates in my sweaty palm. A new message. I tap it and it pops open.

Don't text, it says. And it's from Toby.

Me: *But u r the 1 who gave me this phone*

Toby: *It's for emergencies*

Me: *U never said that*

Toby: *What do u think "buying time" means?*

Me: *Whatever. What's with the panic button?*

Toby: *Don't press the panic button!!*

Me: *What if I'm panicking?*

Toby: *The phone blows up*

Me: *You keep saying that*

Toby: *I'm working out the kinks*

Me: *Great*

The phone vibrates again, kind of violently this time, and just like that the spy directory is gone, taking with it my slim hope of contacting Jennifer. The only people I can text now include Toby and Toby. I want to chuck the phone up the aisle, but I'm afraid it will explode, and I really don't want to drop out of the sky from thirty-nine thousand feet into a cornfield in Indiana before dinner. Instead, I squeeze it really hard. As if it cares.

Me: *Not cool*

Toby: *U r not supposed to have access to the directory anyway*

Me: *Why not?*

Toby: *Not for lower middles*

Me: *Whatever*

Toby: *Just forget about it*

Me: *Whatever*

Toby: *I'm serious*

Me: *I'm getting that*

Toby: *I swear I liked u better when u were just some girl*

Some girl? He's such a jerk! It's not my fault the directory was on the phone. I'm not in charge of spy gear and wonder phones. I think of a number of mean comebacks I could hurl at Toby but choose the silent treatment instead. I power down the phone and slip it into my backpack. So there.

I finally fall asleep when the pilot says we're over Kansas. I've never been so tired. This is not the same fatigue you get from staying up all night at a sleepover. Or reading under the covers with a flashlight until three a.m. This exhaustion is in my bones. It wraps itself around me and hugs me until my eyes close, my mouth hangs open, and I'm pretty sure I drool. I feel loose and twitchy, and at one point Snoring Guy asks me if I'm okay. I nod and pass right back out. Maybe my body thinks if it goes into a deep- enough sleep, it will wake up to a reality that makes more sense. If that's the case, I'm all for it.

I open my eyes when the pilot announces we'll be on the ground in twenty minutes. As directed by the cheery flight attendants, I return my seat back to the upright position. I stow my electronic devices. I put up my tray table. Then I give myself a little pep talk on how this is all going to be just fine. I don't believe any of it, but it seems worth a try.

As I follow signs to baggage claim, I run through how I am to know Bronwyn is Bronwyn. Black jacket. Red flower. Long black hair. Baggage claim. Turtle. I realize I forgot to ask about the specifics of the code-word exchange. Does she whisper it in my ear or something? Just as I'm about to go through the list again, a woman sweeps me up in an unexpected embrace, practically lifting me off my feet.

"You're here!" she says with enthusiasm. "It's so good to see you!"

I study her. Long black hair. Black jacket. Red flower. We're not in baggage claim, but I can see it from here.

"Bronwyn?" I ask tentatively.

"Welcome, Abby!" she replies with a big grin. I don't say anything because I'm waiting for the turtle exchange. We end up staring at each other until Bronwyn asks if I'm feeling okay.

"Yes," I say. "But, you know, is there something you want to tell me?"

She looks puzzled. A strange feeling settles into my stomach. I glance around. She's the only one in the airport wearing a red flower. This is San Francisco. People don't dress up here. This has to be Bronwyn.

"A specific word?" I coax.

"Oh, right! The code word. That's what you're talking about!" She leans in close and whispers "turtle" in my ear. My stomach relaxes.

"Okay?" she says. "We good now?" She glances at her watch and then over her shoulder, dragging me toward an exit in the opposite direction of baggage claim. She's in an awful rush. My stomach does that thing again, but I remember how Mrs. Smith told me my job was to listen to Bronwyn and proceed as directed. So that is what I try to do.

And Bronwyn talks. Boy, does she talk. "Did you have a good trip? Any turbulence? It can be bad this time of year. You got here early, which is great, really great. You have no idea how great. I'm never early. I just parked! I thought I might miss you, and that would be bad, right? Anyway, welcome to California! Did I say that already?"

Some people think all of California is sunny. Malibu is sunny (I've been there), but San Francisco is not. We step out into fog soup. The wind whips my hair as we head for Bronwyn's car. She continues to prattle on about the weather and the 49ers' terrible last season and how this one time she was sailing on the bay and her boat almost sank and how some friend of hers just opened a restaurant and blah, blah, blah.

We climb in the car. Bronwyn pulls a small device that looks like an old-fashioned flip phone from under her seat. She pushes some buttons.

"Got her," she says to someone. "Make sure Mrs. Smith knows she arrived safely." If there's a response, I can't hear it. She shoves the phone back under the seat and peels out of the parking garage.

We drive for several miles in silence. She keeps glancing in the rearview mirror. Visibility is about two feet. I hold on to my seat. Maybe she's used to driving in this fog, but it's freaking me out.

"How much do you know?" Bronwyn asks finally.

I could lie, but why bother? "Nothing."

"They keep you kids so in the dark," she mutters. "It's inconvenient."

I know! Tell me everything! But she doesn't, which is also inconvenient. Instead, she says, "Mrs. Smith believes your presence here in San Francisco will make Jennifer show her hand. Is that what you think?"

"I don't know," I say. No one has asked me what I think about any of this.

"Okay," she says. "Let's just assume they're right. What we need to do is make you visible. Out in the open. Doing things in a very public way until someone makes a move on you and Jennifer jumps in to save you. Then we grab her."

"What?"

Bronwyn throws a glance my way. "That's not how I meant it," she says soothingly. "We want to make sure your mother doesn't come to any harm. She's sitting on some very valuable information. Speaking of which, do you happen to know what it is? Did she ever discuss it with you?"

A minute ago, I liked that she asked me what I thought. Now I'm not so sure. "No," I say, "I have no idea."

"Nothing? Not even a clue?" Bronwyn presses.

"No," I repeat. There's a pause. I can't figure out if it's uncomfortable or not.

"Okay," she says finally. "That's fine. Tomorrow we see what falls out of the trees."

We drive some more. Outside, it's dark, and I can see bits of the city glittering though the fog. Is Jennifer out there somewhere? She's my mother. I should feel her presence. Do I? Nope. Nothing. So far, I'm a terrible spy and possibly not a very good daughter, either.

We pull up in front of a beautiful pale blue house on Jefferson Street in the Marina District of San Francisco. As we climb out of the car, I glimpse the actual marina a few blocks to the north and get a whiff of salty air. Bronwyn glances up and down the street as we take the steps to the front door. Her hand rests lightly on her hip, tucked into her jacket. She hands me a set of keys, nodding for me to open the door.

I do and we enter a vestibule with another door. Bronwyn takes the keys back from me and relaxes her hand. I see the gun in her shoulder holster but try not to stare. The interior door is protected by several keypads as well as a traditional lock. Days seem to go by as I wait for her to enter all the codes and finally unlock the door.

Inside is a tidy room, like any standard living room, with a television and a couch. To the right is a small kitchen, and off to the left is a hallway with several closed doors. Bedrooms maybe. Bronwyn dumps her keys and purse on a narrow hall table.

"Home sweet home," she says. She does not take off her jacket. She does not sit down. Instead, she leads me down the hallway and opens the door to a bedroom. "This is you." Inside is a single twin bed covered with a thin blanket, a nightstand with a lamp, and a desk. There are bars on the window. "Are you hungry?"

I shake my head.

"Bathroom's down the hall," Bronwyn says. "Do you need anything else?"

"Am I supposed to check in with Mrs. Smith?" I ask.

"No, no, I'll take care of it. You get some rest."

She leaves, closing the door behind her. Still clutching my backpack, I sit on the bed and pull my knees to my chest. I wrap my arms around them and squeeze as tight as I can, closing my eyes against unexpected tears.

Chapter 18

THE BLUE SAFE HOUSE. WHERE I HAVE OATMEAL AND MEET A CUTE BOY.

IT'S EIGHT A.M. WHEN I stumble out of my tiny room into the kitchen of the safe house, which looks a little like my kitchen at home in New York, except less ugly. This realization brings with it an intense longing for that drab olive space with the oven that only works when it feels like it and the refrigerator that's as loud as an airplane taking off. I swear if I could be there right now, I would never complain about it again. I click my heels together three times, but nothing happens.

At the table, Bronwyn huddles with a stranger, whispering. When she sees me, the conversation abruptly stops.

"Good morning, Abby," she says brightly. "How'd you sleep?"

Sleep? What? Who is that boy sitting next to you, Bronwyn? I need to know right now. She follows my gaze. Does she roll her eyes? Possibly.

"This is Tom," she says. "He works with me."

Cue the heart-eye emoji and stars twirling around my head. "Hi," I croak. Tom has a mop of blond surfer hair and the bluest eyes I've ever seen. He wears a raggedy Nirvana T-shirt and scuffed-up Vans with a checkerboard print. There's a hole in the knee of his jeans. He's probably fourteen or fifteen, and he's cool. I can just tell.

"Nice to meet you," Tom says. "Hungry?"

Hungry? I'm starving! I slide into the seat across from him.

Bronwyn pushes a healthy portion of oatmeal in my direction. It's covered in all sorts of things I'd normally pitch a fit over—raisins, walnuts, almonds, bananas—but not today. Today I take it with a grin.

"Thank you. This looks delicious." I might giggle.

"Teflon's daughter?" Bronwyn mutters. "Really?"

"Excuse me?" I say.

"Nothing."

I smile like an idiot and dig into my heaping bowl of nutritious oatmeal. I try not to let any dribble down my chin. Bronwyn watches me with something akin to horror. Why is Tom here anyway? He's not a girl.

"Abby," Bronwyn says. "We thought it would be more realistic if you hung around the city with a friend. From the outside, it'll look like two kids having some fun and seeing the sights. Does that make sense?"

A day with Tom? I nod. I grin. I try to compose myself.

"Sounds good to me," says Tom with a wink. I go beet red. In reality, Tom is my babysitter, but who cares? He will be glued to me all day long.

"Now," Bronwyn continues, "you two just do your thing. Wander around. Stay visible. Try not to go inside if you can avoid it. I'll be on you the entire time. Keep your eyes open but also play the part: kids having fun."

Tom gives a mock salute. "Got it," he says.

"Sure," I say. "Great."

"Tom," Bronwyn says. "The tracker?"

"Right." Tom grabs a shabby backpack from the floor behind him and dumps the entire contents on the table, including a half-eaten Clif Bar, an apple core, a calculus textbook, and a green spiral notebook.

"Tracker?" I ask. "Do you plan on losing me?"

"Of course not," says Bronwyn hastily. "But you can never be too prepared."

I must not look convinced, because Tom tells me to relax. "Hey, Abs, we're just two people out having fun."

He called me Abs! I wish I could text my friends. They'd remind me not to act like a dork. I realize not only do I miss them, I almost kind of miss Smith right now. Back at school, it's eleven o'clock and Charlotte and Izumi will be shuffling off to English Composition, dissecting any and all conversations with interesting boys that happened since breakfast. There will be at least some complaining about how much homework there is for World Civilizations, and Quinn will make at least one vain attempt to get Charlotte to fall madly in love with him. And Toby will sit back, watching the whole scene with a look of mild amusement on his face.

"Here we go." Tom's voice brings me back to this strange kitchen table three thousand miles from everything I know. I shake it off. As Mrs. Smith so deftly pointed out, I'm here to do what I'm told, and that's what I'll do. "How about a purple one for you?" Tom throws a purple plastic watch in my direction. I wrap it around my wrist and cinch it tight before realizing it's not a watch at all. It's a small computer screen with two buttons. As soon as it touches my skin, it greets me with a jaunty "Hello" and a mini burst of hearts and stars. I blush. Again.

"Okay," Bronwyn says, "let's get organized and get out there before the day is gone."

A cold sweat blooms across my forehead. What if this all goes horribly awry? Lower Middles the world over will blame me for the failure of the entire operation. That's a lot of pressure. I smile wide and steady myself. I can do this. Tom lays a hand on my shoulder.

"Hey," he says quietly. "Don't worry. We'll protect you. I'll protect you."

I don't swoon. I think seriously about it, but I don't. I take a deep breath. "Okay. I'm ready. Just give me a minute."

In the small bathroom, I brush my teeth and, knowing what I know about the San Francisco wind, pull my hair back into a tight ponytail. I don a Smith School baseball cap and cheap sunglasses. This is me, incognito. I return to the bedroom to find Tom pawing through my backpack of Toby's toys. This is my stuff. Why is he touching it all? More important, he's tapping away on the leopard-print iPhone like he owns the thing.

"Don't play Solitaire!" I shout, making him jump.

"What?"

"Solitaire," I say, grabbing the phone and stuffing it in my jacket pocket. "It blows up."

"You should send it back if it's glitchy," Tom says. He picks up the headphones and examines them. "What's with the pink leopard print anyway? It doesn't seem exactly you."

Does this mean he thinks I'm not girly enough for the phone case? Or that I actually like it? Before I can decide which is worse, he removes the small battery pack and brings it right up close to his face.

"What's this?"

I snatch it from his hands and throw it back in the pack. "A good-luck charm," I say. "Kind of like a rabbit's foot, but not as gross."

I take the pack from the bed and shrug it on. I should probably have kept it out of view. A good spy would have hidden her spyware under the mattress or something. But alas, I'm not a good spy. I'm not even a bad spy. I'm bait.

"We should go," I say. "Bronwyn's waiting."

Plus, I might chicken out any second now.

Chapter 19

SAN FRANCISCO. WHERE TOM AND I PRETEND TO BE FRIENDS.

WE HEAD OUT THE DOOR FIRST. Bronwyn gives us a five-minute head start. Traveling west, we hit Broderick Street and turn right. The sun is bright and the fog that devoured the city last night has receded. The bay glistens like it's sprinkled with diamond dust. We walk a paved path alongside a marina, where gleaming white yachts sway and tug at their mooring lines. I take a deep inhale of the salty air.

"Have you ever been here?" Tom asks. "San Francisco?"

"Once," I say, remembering.

It was one of Jennifer's courier trips where she dragged me out of bed in the middle of the night and plopped us on an airplane to an unknown destination that turned out to be here. We met a man in Golden Gate Park by the Conservatory of Flowers, a building that looks like a glass wedding cake. I wanted to buy tickets and go inside because a giant banner over the entry promised a thrilling exhibit about man-eating plants. Jennifer said I had to wait until later.

"But I'm missing school!" I protested. "Shouldn't I be doing something educational at least? Man-eating plants are educational!"

"Meat-eating plants," she corrected. "We're waiting for someone."

"That's not educational."

"Patience is a virtue."

"Not one of mine," I grumbled. I entertained myself by hanging upside down on the guardrail to the stairs, much to the horror of the many visitors tromping into the conservatory to see the carnivorous plants. Meanwhile, Jennifer scanned all their faces, back and forth, constantly and continuously. If she objected to my acting like a wild monkey, she didn't mention it.

We waited a long time. The someone was an hour late, and this made Jennifer tense. I could tell because she gnawed on her cuticles, and she only did that when she was thinking really hard or freaking out about something.

And if this person didn't show up soon, she was in danger of running out of fingers to chew.

But he did finally arrive, and Jennifer handed him an envelope, which he took without a word and quickly left. The entire exchange took exactly ten seconds. My mother then flashed me a bright smile and said we could go see the plants.

Tom's voice breaks the spell. "San Francisco's the best city in the world," he says with a grin. He's cute but deluded.

"Have you even been to New York?" I ask, incredulous.

"Yeah." He sniffs. "One time. It was hot and smelled bad."

"You can't make up your mind about a place after a single visit. There's just no way."

"Well, you've only been here once!" he protests.

"And I haven't made any decisions about it one way or another!" I bark back.

We reach a stalemate and walk on in silence. Soon we arrive at a wide, sandy path separated from the bay by beach and scrub. The waves roll in smoothly, and I pause to enjoy them. I don't get to the ocean much, but in this city it's everywhere.

The walking path is crowded with people. Some are clearly tourists, puzzling over maps and freezing in the stiff cold wind. There are moms with strollers and joggers and more tourists on bikes, careening this way and that as if riding irritated broncos. It's not the kind of walk where you can lose yourself in the scenery unless you want to get run over. Even the moms in their brightly colored workout wear are intensely focused—baby strolling as competitive sport. I keep to the edge of the path and put Tom between all the dangerous people and me.

Plus, I have the added paranoia of thinking each and every person we pass wants to kidnap me or kill me or, I don't know, do something terrible. I avert my eyes to avoid showing my fear. Tom clears his throat. It sounds like an attempt to reboot our conversation.

"So I hear you're new to this whole thing," he says.

I laugh. I can't help it. "'New' is probably the right word for it. Last week I was a normal Lower Middle, I mean seventh grader, and now, well, now here I am."

"Jennifer Hunter's a legend," he says.

Oh no, not again. Not the *Jennifer was a superhero until you came along and wrecked it* soliloquy. I'm not sure I can take it. Unfortunately, Tom sees my clenched-jaw silence as a sign to go on talking about Jennifer.

"There was one time," he continues, "when she actually ran the length of a moving train on the roof, chasing a guy. It was in Switzerland or something. Going up a mountain!

I know you see that in the movies, but do you know how hard it is to do in real life and not die?"

"No," I say with a grimace. "I don't. Because I can honestly say I've never thought about it before right this minute."

"Well, it's impossible! Only Teflon could pull that off. And she got the guy, of course."

"Of course."

"Anyway, I'm not supposed to talk to you about her, but I can't help it. She was cool back in the day."

"Apparently."

"So what's she like now?" he asks. "What's it like seeing her all the time?"

I want to scream, but I fear that in this wind the effect will be utterly wasted. "She's fine," I say. "Normal. She likes movies." I hope this is enough. "Did you know that as soon as they finish painting the Golden Gate Bridge, they start all over again at the beginning?"

"What?"

"Trivia," I say, "about your city."

"They're putting up a net to catch the jumpers too," Tom says. "It's going to ruin the bridge." He goes on about San Francisco politics for a while, and I watch the waves as we walk along.

We stop fifteen minutes later at the Warming Hut, a small bay-side building selling sandwiches, coffee, and hot chocolate, plus postcards, books, and toys to frozen visitors. It's crowded with bodies, and Tom takes my hand. I experience an unexpected tingle up my arm. Maybe I can forgive him for dissing New York.

We push up to the counter and order two hot chocolates with whipped cream. A little kid crashes into my legs and I flinch.

"Don't worry," Tom says. "You're fine." I couldn't tell if he was talking to me or the kid.

We take the hot chocolate and walk out onto a wide pier that extends into the bay. A bunch of bored-looking fishermen cast lines into the water. At the far end, we sit on the pier's edge, our legs dangling over the side. Sailboats and a dozen kite surfers cruise on the icy water. I've never seen a kite surfer before. They bounce off the surface as if untethered from gravity, holding on to a giant kite, feet strapped into a modified surfboard. They move much faster than the seagulls circling continuously overhead, zipping out of sight in an instant.

"Have you ever done that?" I ask, gesturing to one of the kite surfers.

"No," Tom says with a shiver.

"Have you seen Bronwyn since we left?"

"No. But don't worry. You're not supposed to see her. Drink your hot chocolate."

I take a sip. "Thanks."

"I'm on an expense account," Tom says with a grin.

"Can I ask you something?"

"Sure. Shoot."

"What do you know about all of this?"

"Your mom being gone, you mean?"

I nod, fearing my voice will crack.

"Well," he says, "Suzie called me yesterday and asked if I could do this today. Usually, I have more lead time when they send me out, so I was kind of surprised."

"Who?"

"Bronwyn, I mean," he says quickly. He casts his eyes down, away from mine. My stomach tightens uncomfortably. He definitely said Suzie. I try to keep my face neutral as I race through possibilities. The obvious answer is the Ghost's people have kidnapped me and intend to use me for the same purposes the Center did. But the Bronwyn at the airport had the flower! And the password! Sure, she forgot to give it to me right away, but she knew it. But then again, she wasn't at baggage claim and hustled me out of the airport in an awful hurry. What if I'd checked a suitcase? Suddenly, I have a terrible thought. *Somebody's sold me out.*

But before I can latch onto this idea and totally freak out, my eyes are drawn to one of the kite surfers that dot the bay. Most of the surfers are middle-aged men, soft around the middle, with wet suits squeezing them a bit too tightly. Sausages with helmets, tufts of wet gray hair sticking out every which way. But not this guy. This guy wears a neoprene mask and looks like something out of a horror movie. He executes an amazing one-hundred-eighty-degree turn, bouncing over the waves, leaving a wake of spray. He's moving so fast, flying through the air, ten feet above the water now on a hydrofoil board and coming right at us.

And then he's on me like a seagull on an ice-cream cone and I'm dragged away onto the bay, still clutching my hot chocolate, the remaining whipped cream flying into the wind.

Chapter 20

WHERE I GET AN UP-CLOSE VIEW OF SAN FRANCISCO BAY.

WHAT'S FUNNY IS I DON'T SCREAM. It's like when Veronica was beating me up and I started thinking about other things. Well, right now I'm thinking how beautiful the bay looks rushing by at an insane speed beneath my feet. Sure, I'm terrified. And freezing. But still, Alcatraz glimmers in the faint sunlight and the waves are dark blue rippling silk.

The man has me around the waist and he's holding on tight. If he lets go, he'll run me over. We're moving fast, so much faster than it appears from land. So wrestling free is not an option. I crane my neck around to catch a glimpse of him.

"Stop doing that!" he yells. It's hard to hear with the wind in my ears.

"Doing what?"

"Wiggling."

"I'm not wiggling. Believe me."

"You are. Stop it." His voice is strained. It must not be so easy to hold on to me and not lose control of the kite or the board. We head toward the Golden Gate Bridge. It's an incredible sight, and that's probably why in disaster movies it's always the first thing to get blown up. From this angle, it looms large.

The purple tracker slides down my wrist. If Bronwyn is not Bronwyn, then Tom is not Tom. I have terrible luck with boys. The cute ones are either not interested (think Quinn) or playing for Team Evil. Do Fake Bronwyn and Tom work for the Ghost? Are they in competition with the Ghost? Mrs. Smith said there would be others.

With freezing fingers, I peel the watch off my wrist and let it fly away into the bay. I've been kidnapped from my kidnappers by a kite surfer. This has got to be some kind of first. I come up with a quick plan: survive and escape.

"Where are you taking me?" I shout. *Japan? Hawaii? There's a whole lot of nothing once you pass under that bridge.*

"Somewhere."

"That's not superhelpful," I say.

"Stop talking," he grunts. I'm guessing he's working up a good sweat in all that neoprene. A ferry shuttling visitors from San Francisco to Alcatraz passes on our right. They look at us. Some of them point.

"Wave," the man instructs. "Act like you're having fun."

The passengers wave back. Don't any of these people know weird when they see it? The ferry slips out of view and we draw closer to the bridge. My feet are soaked and tingle painfully in the cold.

"So we're headed west," I say, sounding oddly conversational in light of the circumstances. "Where are you planning on landing?"

"It's not called 'landing.'"

"I don't know anything about kite surfing," I say. "Actually, this is my first time. So what's it called when you, you know, stop? You do know how to stop, don't you?"

"You have a lot of questions."

"Wouldn't you?"

"I guess."

"How much longer?" I ask. "I'm freezing."

"I'm not exactly having much fun myself." He switches arms so the one around my waist is now controlling the kite. I think he groans.

"Sorry," I say. "You could just let me go. I mean, once we're on land and all. "

"Not an option."

I didn't think so, but sometimes when you ask for things politely, you get them. We pass under the bridge and head north along the jagged coastline of the Marin Headlands. Ahead is a beach tucked into a small cove. Even though I can see the San Francisco skyline over my right shoulder, there's something about this location that feels remote.

Our landing, or whatever it's called, is not exactly graceful. We're ten feet above the water when the man unclips his feet from the board but doesn't neutralize the sail, so we literally fly through the air and crash on the narrow, sandy strip. My ankles buckle with the impact. My kidnapper grunts, and I realize he's working hard not to fall over and crush me. I scramble out from under him. He untangles himself, pulls off his mask, and swabs his sweaty face with the red bandanna tied around his neck. A big blue Rip Curl logo strains across his wide chest. He looks like he might burst out of the wet suit any second now.

"I thought that would be easier," Rip Curl wheezes, bending at the waist, hands on knees. "I do CrossFit six times a week. I compete! And win! This sucks."

"Are you okay?" I ask.

"Yeah," he says miserably. "Listen, kid. Don't try anything funny. I may look like I just do the heavy lifting around here, but I'm no dummy."

"If you say so," I say. Rip Curl remains hunched over. I take the opportunity to do something funny and slip the super-iPhone out of my zippered pocket. Hot water? Rubber bullet? Or maybe I'll just text him to death?

I decide on the hot water, recognizing that if this doesn't work I will be in hot water. Rip straightens up and sees the iPhone in my hand.

"Hey!" he yells. "Give me that! What did I tell you?" As he lunges for me, the sleeve of his wet suit slides up an inch. His forearm is inked.

"Wait!" I shriek, hitting a seriously high octave. Rip Curl jumps back, eyes wide.

"What?"

"Your tattoo. What is it?"

He looks utterly confused, but he's a man used to taking orders. He peels up the wet-suit sleeve to reveal an awkward falcon on a surfboard. Talk about poor choices.

"Not a triangle," I murmur.

"A triangle, did you say? Well, I might be crazy, but I'm not that crazy. He brands his people like cattle. Only crazies ride the crazy train with that crazy dude, you hear what I'm saying?"

Yes. I can now take comfort in the fact that there are two separate criminal elements out to get me, Team Triangle and Team Surfing Falcon. "Crazy people only," I say with a smile.

"Yeah. Now give me that phone."

Sorry. No way. I aim it level with his face. "Toby is cool. Spray bottle!" I yell. The phone makes a high-pitched gurgling sound and practically leaps out of my hands, but a stream of boiling water emerges from the top, directly into the eyes of my very surprised captor.

He shrieks. "My eyes! What did you do? Acid! I can't see!" He hops around on one foot like he just stubbed his toe, the palms of his hands covering his face.

Without thinking, I kick him where it counts—I didn't grow up in New York City for nothing. Rip Curl falls to his knees, pawing at his eyes. I kick him again and run, shouting back over my shoulder, "It's just hot water! Don't be such a baby!"

I dash up the rickety stairs leading from the deserted beach to a narrow walking path above. Charging down the path, trying not to fall on my face, I frantically hit the radio icon on the phone until Toby answers.

"Abby?"

"Yes! It's me!"

"Where have you been?" he yells, frantic. "Why didn't you answer any of my messages? We finally heard from Bronwyn and she said you never got off the plane. Everyone is looking for you!"

That's because apparently I went home with someone named Suzie who tried to lull me into complacency with a cute boy! I'm embarrassed to be such an easy target. As for Toby's messages, I remember Tom with my phone this morning. Was he erasing messages? Of course he was! Down on the beach I see Rip Curl struggling to his feet. I start to run.

"What are you doing?" Toby yells. "I can't see you, and I can barely hear you. Something must be up with my connection."

"But your connection is foolproof," I gasp.

"No connection is foolproof," Toby says. "You sound out of breath."

"Well, that's because I'm running for my life! I was just kidnapped by a kite surfer, but I used the hot water on him and—"

"So the water worked? Cool. I never got around to field-testing it."

"No! Not cool! What do I do?"

"I don't know. Keep running?"

That is so not helpful.

"Okay," Toby says. "I've got Mrs. Smith on the other line. She says . . . keep running. I'm zeroing in on your location. You can't stand still for a second, can you?"

"Are you insane? Why would you even ask me that?" I charge along the path, race up about fifty wooden steps, and finally hit the paved road. I glance left and right. *Now what?*

"I've got you on the sensors," Toby says. I take off down the road. "No!" he shouts. "The other way."

I pivot and set off in the other direction, throwing a quick glance over my shoulder. I'm keeping good distance between Rip Curl and me, but it won't last. The reason I didn't try out for the cross-country team in the fall is I hate running and I'm not that good at it. My entire body is drenched in sweat, my quads burn, and my heart feels like it's going to burst right out of my chest.

But I keep running.

"Mrs. Smith says she's sending someone to get you," Toby says. "Can you hang in there?"

I stop running because I'm about to throw up. The world around me swims in lazy circles. I bet Veronica can run clear to the top of this hill, and then drop and do fifty push-ups on the summit. I need more exercise. Fewer breakfast donuts and more exercise. I might die before I get to act on this resolution, though.

I'm doing my best not to hyperventilate when Toby says, "Okay. So, Abby?"

"What?"

"Time to get moving again. Your friend is coming up fast."

"Rip Curl is not my friend," I wheeze.

"Cut across the scrub," Toby says, remote piloting me like I'm a human drone. "Hard right. It's bushwhacking time."

"I don't even know what that means!" I shout.

"Off road. Disappear in those bushes!" I careen off into the low scrub. This is a harsh environment, and these are hard plants, covered in spikes and razor-sharp leaves. They slice at my legs and grab my jacket. I push on. "Now get down low and stop moving," Toby says.

"Gladly," I say, dropping behind a bush and making myself small. I try to quiet my breathing, but it's not easy. Soon, I hear footsteps on the road. They grow louder. From my hiding place I see Rip Curl jogging along, panting. He stops perpendicular to me.

Blend with the bushes. Become one with the foliage. *Oh, please don't see me!*

"No sign of her," Rip Curl says into his phone. "I don't know. How am I supposed to know? She shot me in the face with acid, okay? I might be blind in one eye! Besides, none of this was my plan. It was yours. Where are you, anyway? I'm freezing."

Moments later a black SUV trundles down the winding road and stops beside the man. The rear passenger door swings open, and I catch a glimpse of a hand, a decidedly female hand wearing a big diamond ring that actually glints in the pale sun.

"Get in," says a voice. Imagine Tinker Bell but much larger and not so taken with Peter Pan.

"Sorry, boss," says Rip Curl, hanging his head.

The hand beckons him forward, and the voice warns him not to get the seats wet. I pick this moment to have my very first exercise-induced asthma attack.

Chapter 21

THE HEADLESS PRIUS.

GASPING AND WHEEZING ARE the least of my problems. I've blown my cover. Tinker Bell shoves Rip Curl back out of the monster SUV.

"Get her!" she yells. Rip Curl spots me immediately and starts plowing through the scrub in my direction with great enthusiasm. His boss is watching. Clearly, he wants to impress her. I would think she'd have been plenty impressed with the kite-surfing bit. I'm on my feet, running full-out again. My lungs are on fire. Rip Curl draws closer. I stumble. Can Toby hear me? Does he know what's going on?

Jennifer liked to talk about self-reliance. "When

things are really crazy," she'd say, "that's when you need to have the most confidence in yourself and be bold even if it's scary." Now, I thought she was talking about crossing the street against the light or muscling through a hard set of math problems. But she was probably talking about running away from bad guys. I can't rely on Toby to help me from three thousand miles away. I'm by myself.

I get back on my feet just as Rip Curl's hand grazes my ankle. I kick hard and sprint for the road. In the distance, a black Prius flies in my direction. That must be my ride. That had *better* be my ride. With an extra burst of speed, I race toward the oncoming car.

But the car has no driver. Yes, it's coming toward me at eighty miles an hour and it's not careening off the road, but the driver's seat is empty. Just last week Izumi was reading to me about Google inventing the self-driving car. She was superexcited by the idea. I am not. But beggars can't be choosers.

The car skids to a stop in front of me. I throw myself into the backseat and slam the door just as Rip Curl arrives. He pulls on the door handle, but it's locked. The Prius peels out. Yes, they can do that. I know. I find it surprising too.

The SUV comes up fast behind us. The Prius rips down the road, banking so hard around the curves I slam into the door. We make another tight turn, and I'm thrown in the opposite direction. I hit my head on the window. I can't even yell at the maniac driving to slow down, because there is no one, maniac or otherwise, at the wheel.

The SUV is right on our bumper. I wedge myself in the foot well and brace against the driver's seat. Another hard right and I swear we are up on two wheels. Suddenly, a loud explosion from the rear of the car, like a backfire, and a sharp clattering sound. A dense acidic smell fills the air. I gag and pop my head up enough to catch a glimpse of a cloud of dark smoke behind us. And the road appears littered with shiny metal spikes.

The SUV emerges from the cloud of smoke and hits the spikes. It careens off the road and comes to an abrupt stop in the bushes. The Prius takes off like a shot. I'm thrown from the foot well and back into the window, but this time I tuck my head down by my knees and make myself into a tight ball.

If I live through this, I will be thrilled.

The rough ride continues for another five minutes, by which point I feel as if I've had a turn in the clothes dryer. Finally, I crawl back into the seat and glance out the window. We're on a multilane freeway with the bay to the east. I have no idea where I'm going. I pull out the iPhone to try Toby, but my battery is dead. No, no, no! I dig around in the pack for the charger but come up with something much more sinister: another purple tracking device. Tom must have slipped it into my pack this morning. Is there anyone who doesn't think I can lead them to whatever Jennifer has? Mrs. Smith, Toby, Lotus Man, Tinker Bell, Rip Curl, Fake Bronwyn, Tom. The list is getting long. If you had asked me last week if I had enemies, I would have said no. Sure, Veronica and her pack of mean girls are, well, mean, but they're like that to anyone. This is different. These people want to do me harm.

Before I can full-out panic, there's a sudden commotion in the trunk, and the rear passenger seat beside me flattens to reveal a contorted Tom. I'm in a driverless car with the enemy. Quickly, I stuff the phone and the battery back in my pocket, out of sight. Tom unfurls a long leg and an arm, and finally the rest of his body comes out of the small opening and practically into my lap.

"Hey!" I shout. But I keep my face neutral. He doesn't know that I know he's a bad guy. And being as he appears to be in charge of the self-driving car, there is no need for him to know that I know he's a bad guy.

"Hey, yourself," Tom grumbles. "Can you pull my leg

straight? I have a hamstring cramp." He throws his leg over me and winces. I grab his tennis shoe and push down on his knee. He howls.

"Well, don't whine," I say. "You asked for help."

"I've been in there for an hour. I don't think I'm ever going to be a fighter pilot."

"Was that a possibility?"

"Not really." He grins. "I'm glad you're okay."

"Who was that who took me?" I ask. I was instructed to do as I was told and not ask questions, but the situation has changed and I need intel.

"We don't know," Tom says, all innocent. "It's probably safe to say we're not the only ones after Teflon. It's a good thing I threw that extra tracker in your bag, right?"

"Oh yeah," I say. "Totally." How bad would it be if I unlocked the door and kicked him out of a car moving at seventy miles an hour? Bad. Really bad. I subtly try the handle, but it's locked, and there's no obvious way to unlock it. This confirms my status as hostage. I'm having a big day, and it's not even lunchtime.

Tom grins at me. I grin back. We're both lying.

"What is this car, anyway?" I ask, hoping he'll spend the next hour gushing like boys do about cool toys while I formulate a bombproof escape plan. But he won't move on.

"I'm really sorry I lost you back there," he says. "We didn't expect that."

"So where's Bronwyn?" I ask. *I mean Suzie, you traitor.*

"She's at the safe house. Up in the mountains. That's where we're headed now. It's impossible to find."

"Of course. A safe house. To, you know, keep me safe."

"Exactly! We won't let anyone else get to you."

Because you got me first and I bet you're making sure Jennifer knows it. "I feel so much better," I say.

"Hey," he says with calculated casualness, "can I see that phone of yours again? It was really cool."

Are you kidding me? Do you think I was born yesterday? "I lost it on the water when I lost my wrist tracker," I say. "Total drag."

Tom ripples with tension. I can't tell if he believes me or not. I wait for him to make a move, unsure what my options are in this close environment. Veronica never mentioned how to beat someone up in a space the size of a soda can. But the moment passes and he relaxes.

"So, the car?" I ask again. And he starts telling me all about it. That's how we spend the long drive to the mountains.

At some point I fall asleep, because before I know it, the

Headless Prius rolls to a smooth stop on a freshly plowed driveway with fifteen-foot walls of snow on either side. Outside, it's a winter wonderland.

"Hey, Sleeping Beauty," Tom says. "Wake up. We're here." Way back this morning, when I thought Tom was cute and not evil, the Sleeping Beauty comment would have made me blush. But now it's just plain creepy. Out the front windshield I see an A-frame house. There are no obvious neighbors. I may as well have landed on Mars.

"I don't have snow boots," I say flatly. "Or a toothbrush." Or clean underwear. Or pajamas. I don't have the book I'm supposed to read for Chinese History. I'm totally unprepared for being held hostage in the snowy mountains, and my nap in the car has left me cranky.

"Stop worrying, Abby."

Easy for him to say. I climb out, careful not to take a header on the icy driveway. The weak sun drops fast, and I shiver. My feet are still damp from the kite-surfing incident. The house is nestled into a crop of lodge pines, all dusted white with snow. Smoke rises in a plume from the chimney. It's a lovely scene straight off a holiday card, and it chills me to the bone. How is anyone supposed to find me here? Priority one is charging my phone. Well, priority one is making sure they don't find and take my phone and then charging it.

Up close, I notice steel bars over the windows again and multiple locks on the front door. I swallow, my mouth dry. To the right of the door, carved into one of the massive facade stones, is a symbol. A triangle, each thick segment a different color, just like Lotus Man's tattoo. Down in the catacombs, Toby got really excited when I mentioned the triangle tattoo, but of course he never bothered to explain why it was important. In this information-packed universe, I am clueless.

Inside, Fake Bronwyn waits for us in the high-ceilinged family room, complete with rustic exposed beams and an enormous stone fireplace. Surreptitiously, I scan the rocks to see if maybe this fireplace is a secret passage to someplace else, like pretty much anywhere but here.

"Abby, you look exhausted." Fake Bronwyn appears and gives me a hug. I plaster a smile on my face.

"Yeah," I say. "Tired." She takes me by the shoulders and gives me a serious look.

"That must have been scary," she says. "And I'm really, really sorry it happened, especially on my watch. I promised Mrs. Smith I'd take care of you."

You did not! You stole me from Mrs. Smith! I keep smiling, although I have to grind my teeth to do it. "Maybe I should call her?" I suggest.

"Oh, let me take care of that," Fake Bronwyn says quickly, releasing me. "I'm supposed to update her anyway."

I bet you are. "Is there someplace I can lie down?" I say with a fake yawn. If I can't find a way to get this phone charged, I'm sunk. I refuse to think about what they plan on doing to me to get my mother's attention.

"Of course," Bronwyn says. "Tom, will you show Abby the small bedroom in the front, upstairs?"

Tom leads me upstairs. There appears to be only one way out of this place, and that's the way we came in. With all the barred windows, this house makes a very scenic prison.

"What's with the windows?" I ask as we make our way down a narrow hallway.

"Bears," Tom says.

"Bears?"

"Yeah. They're a serious problem up here in the Sierra Nevada. They get into houses and really mess stuff up."

"I bet."

The room is small and spare, just like the room in the San Francisco house. Clearly, whoever runs this outfit doesn't allow for a decorating budget. I drop my pack on the bed and give another fake yawn, this time with an exaggerated arm stretch.

"Well, thanks for rescuing me," I say, nudging Tom back into the hallway. "I'm going to take a quick nap." I shut the door in his face.

Quickly, I pull the phone and charger from my pocket, thinking Mrs. Smith is right. No one suspects a kid. As soon as the phone is plugged in, I press the on button, but nothing happens. The phone is so dead. Here's that patience thing again. And still not my strong suit.

I tuck the second purple tracker under the thin mattress and stretch out on the bed. I slide the phone and the quick charger under my back so they are both out of sight. So what do I know for sure? This house, and therefore Bronwyn and Tom, Lotus Man, and Mystery Man are all connected. And it's probably safe to say that that they all work for someone who has the same idea about me that Mrs. Smith does. Is this someone the Ghost or one of the Ghost's competitors? Well, it doesn't matter, because one thing is clear: Their theory is flawed. Whether Jennifer knows I'm here or not, she is not going to save me.

I'm on my own and I'm getting out of here no matter what.

Chapter 22

WHERE THINGS GO WELL (UNTIL THEY DON'T).

I SLEEP FOR A WHILE and when I wake up, I notice my backpack is in a different spot. Someone came in here and dug through it. But my phone is still tucked into the back of my pants, and now it's charged. I sneak a peek down the hallway to make sure no one is around. Voices drift from another room, so I figure I'm safe. Quietly, I close the door and press my back to it. When I pull up the radio icon, perfectly connected now, I see Toby's sleeping face squished against his laptop camera. He's down in the catacombs, and the view of his nose is particularly impressive.

"Wake up!" I whisper. Three thousand miles away, Toby jolts to life and rubs his eyes. When he sees me, he shouts,

"Where have you been, Abby?" I muffle the phone under my armpit.

"Be quiet!" I say.

"The car came for you in the Headlands," he says. "Where were you?"

"Well, I got in the first car that came along," I hiss. "It was Tinker Bell or the Headless Prius."

"I have no idea what you're talking about," he says. "Why did you turn off the phone?"

"It died."

"I told you to keep it charged," he huffs. "I thought you were dead."

Is he kidding me with this? I'm trapped in a mountain prison with two lunatics, and he's giving me grief about charging my phone? "If you don't help me get out of here, your wish of me being dead might come true."

He visibly bristles. His jaw tightens. "I didn't say I wished that."

"Just get me out of here!" I whisper-shout.

"Hold on, will you?" he says. "I can't get a definite location on you. Must be interference."

"This system of yours really stinks."

"I'm going to ignore that," he says. "Anyway, the plan has changed. They're coming to get you."

"'They'?" I'm not sure I like the sound of that.

"Mrs. Smith and Veronica." I was right. I don't like the sound of that.

"Great," I mutter.

"Okay," he says. "So instructions are to sit tight and wait."

"No."

"No?"

"Every time I follow the instructions, bad things happen. Help me get out of here. I'll take my chances with the bears."

"The bears are hibernating," Toby says. "It's winter. Instructions are to wait."

"You sound like a robot," I say.

"I do not," he says. "You just don't like what I'm telling you to do."

I don't want to talk to him because he's a brat, but I also don't want to be alone in Popsicle-ville, so I change the subject. "There's a triangle here," I say.

"Huh?"

"Remember I told you that Lotus Man had a triangle tattoo on his forearm? And then you guys just kind of forgot to tell me what it means? So what does it mean? Because it's on a plaque outside the front door."

"Are you sure?"

"Yes, I'm sure."

"That's a problem," he says, grim.

"What does it mean?"

"All of the Ghost's people supposedly have an equilateral triangle tattoo. All sides are equal, meaning everyone in his network needs everyone else. Until he's mad at you. Then it's pretty much game over."

Did he need to tell me that while I'm trapped in the crazy man's house? No, he did not. "Thanks for that," I say.

"Oh, don't worry about it," Toby says quickly. "You'll be fine."

"No, I won't. When they realize Jennifer's not going to swoop in here and rescue me and their plan is a total failure, then what? You think they're just going to call me a taxi and let me go home? You live in a fantasy world, Toby."

Before Toby can work up an answer to that, I hear heavy footsteps coming down the hallway. "I have to go," I say, and power down the phone. I can't risk it beeping and singing and chirping at me. This phone is my lifeline. I shove it down the back of my pants and throw myself onto the bed. I pull my knees up to my chest and close my eyes. Sleeping just like a baby. Tom gently pushes open the door and peers in.

"Abby?"

I open one eye just a crack, give a fake yawn, and curl back into a ball. Tom sits on the side of the bed and rests a hand on my shoulder.

"Abby?" he says again. "I thought I heard you talking. Do you need something?"

I yawn again. "Nope," I say. "Just sleeping up here. That's all." The phone digs uncomfortably into my back, but I don't dare adjust it.

"Bronwyn made some spaghetti," he says, "if you're hungry." The truth is I'm starving. I haven't had anything to eat since this morning's oatmeal, and running for your life burns a lot of calories.

"Has anyone talked to Mrs. Smith?" I ask as innocently as possible.

Tom shifts on the bed, removing his hand from my shoulder. Does he look sheepish, embarrassed? I'd like to think so.

"Yes," he mumbles. "We're supposed to sit tight and wait. You'll be safe here. This isn't an easy house to get into." Or out of, I'm sure.

I get out of bed, making a big production of stretching and rubbing my eyes, and we head to the kitchen for pasta. Bronwyn's pasta is like her oatmeal: full of all sorts of nutritious and unidentifiable green stuff. It's a little strange that she is presumably putting me in harm's way but feeding me healthy meals. Why not chain me in a corner and throw crusts of bread at me every twelve hours?

I eat the pasta because it's delicious and I'm hungry. Plus, I'll need energy for my escape. I could be walking for days out there in the frozen tundra. During the meal, I ask lots of questions about the house in what I hope is a subtle way. When they start looking at me funny, I stop and inquire about the weather.

This works out better. As Bronwyn and Tom go on about the megadrought and extreme temperature fluctuations, I take the opportunity to scan the room. Over the sink is a small rectangular window without bars. Probably because it's too small for an adult to squeeze through. But not a kid. I grin. I'm going through that window. I don't know how or when or what will happen on the other side, but at least I have an idea of how to implement step one of my escape plan.

I'm so pleased with my progress I help myself to another heaping bowl of spaghetti and green stuff, after which we shuffle to the family room to watch television like this is all so very normal. After an hour, Bronwyn sends us to bed. I lie on the thin mattress and pinch my thigh every time my eyes threaten to close. I will not fall asleep. I will stay awake and wait for an opportunity to make my move out that window.

My thigh burns and stings, but eventually I hear Bronwyn honking like a goose and Tom muttering in his sleep. They obviously don't see me as a flight risk. The coast is as clear as it's going to get.

Slowly and cautiously, I slip on my backpack and tiptoe from my room. I take the stairs, quiet as a mouse. By the time I reach the kitchen, my heart races and my palms are damp. Can I really pull this off?

I climb quietly up on the counter and peer out the small window. A full moon casts long shadows. The house is built into a mountain, so although I'm on the first floor, I'm still twenty five feet above the ground, which means I can't jump. An escape cannot be called successful if it ends with me as a heap of broken bones.

To the left of the window, about five feet away, is the big wooden back deck. There are a few snow-covered lounge chairs and a barbecue grill still out there. Maybe in summer, when she's not busy kidnapping innocent people, Fake Bronwyn enjoys hanging on the deck admiring the scenery? Either way, I can't make it to the deck from the window, and I can't jump.

But before true despair sets in, I notice a long gutter pipe that goes from roof to ground. It's between the small window and the deck. If I can get out the window and grab on to the pipe, I can get close enough to swing over the rail of the deck, and then I'm home free. Unless the pipe detaches from the house or I fall or Fake Bronwyn catches me, in which case I'm back to the heap-of-broken-bones situation.

Opening the window takes some effort and each time metal scrapes metal, I wince, sure I'm about to be busted for what I'm starting to think is my very lame attempt to flee. Finally, the window pops open. Leaning my arm out, I fling the backpack onto the deck. It lands with a *thud*. I should be so lucky.

I give myself a quick pep talk. *You can totally do this, Abby! It's time to get out of the Ghost's house! Piece of cake! Jennifer could do this with her eyes closed and her hands tied behind her back! Or at least that's what everyone seems to think. Go, go, go!*

It still takes me a minute to actually climb through the window. Back at McKinsey House I could cling to my bedsheets. This feels more freestyle. My heart pounds so loudly I worry it will wake the terrible twosome sleeping upstairs. I slide my legs, one at a time, through the window. Holding on for dear life, I work my torso over the window ledge so I'm hanging by my elbows.

Balanced precariously, I swing my right leg out to try to catch the pipe. I miss. My arms start to twitch, and despite the freezing temperature and my chattering teeth, I break out in a cold sweat. This was a bad idea, but pulling myself back in the window is no longer an option. I kick my leg out again, harder. This time, I get purchase on the pipe. But it makes a loud *clank*, and I freeze, listening for footsteps in the house. All remains quiet. To grab onto the pipe Koalabear-style, I first dangle from the window ledge with my fingers. This is followed by a lunge for the pipe. If I miss, splat.

Everything goes in slow motion. I let go on the window and pull with my leg. Desperately, I grab the pipe with both arms and hug it for dear life. It's a second before I realize I'm fine. Not slipping. Not falling. Just clinging. And I'm halfway to the deck!

I stretch my arm out for the icy deck railing. I could really use some gloves. *Don't think about the cold, just hold on.* In an instant, I'm hanging there for dear life. Inch by inch, I pull my legs up until I can slide between the rails, landing safely on solid ground.

I roll over in the snow, grab my backpack, and search for the stairs down from the deck. Except there aren't any.

I may have gotten out of the house, but now I'm trapped on the deck. I lean out over the deck railing. The structure is supported by several upright wooden columns. The only way down is by way of wooden column.

I stuff the contents of my backpack into my jacket pockets and unzip the pack entirely. Climbing over the deck railing, I crouch low and wrap the unzipped pack around the top of a column and then wrap my arms and legs around the pack so I can slide down without a world of splintery pain. My arms ache, but I hug that column like we're BFFs and slowly shimmy my way to the ground.

When I finally land in the snow, I want to cry with joy. Quickly, I make my way around the house toward the road. I'm just about there when I hear, "Abby? What are you doing out here?"

This is a problem.

Chapter 23

WHERE I GO SWIMMING BY THE LIGHT OF THE MOON.

GOING FOR A WALK. *Getting some fresh air. Stretching my legs. Sleepwalking. Howling at the moon. Escaping?* In the end I stand there mute. It was going so well! Why is Tom out here all of a sudden?

"Um," I finally manage. "I thought I might just, you know, get some air."

"I told you about the bears," he says, his gaze falling on my pack. A minute ago he looked sleepy. Not anymore. He takes a step toward me. I step back. He's not wearing shoes and begins hopping from foot to foot on the icy ground.

This makes me think I can run.

"Abby?" he says.

It's now or never. I turn and sprint, scrambling over a snowbank and crashing down the other side into the woods. I get to my feet and push deeper into the trees, but it's slow going. Thigh-high snow in tennis shoes and jeans is a challenge.

"Suzie!" I hear Tom shouting. "She's getting away!"

I reach another wall of snow and haul myself up and over it, spilling out onto a narrow empty road. In the moonlight, I cast long eerie shadows. At least it's easier to run on the road, but it's slippery, and twice I go down hard. My knees sing with pain.

A little ways down the road, I spy a rack storing several canoes and kayaks for the winter. Beyond the rack is a frozen lake. Only when I'm safely tucked in among the hibernating boats do I realize I've left a trail of tracks in the fresh snow, like a giant neon sign announcing, *I am right here. Come and get me!*

So maybe I don't get an A+ in Escaping on Foot in the Frozen Tundra? Before I can come up with a fix or call Toby and ask him what I should do, Suzie (at least I know that now) and Tom come running down the road right toward me.

"Why didn't you grab her?" Suzie yells at Tom.

"I was barefoot!"

"So what? I'm not paying you to be a wimp about your feet."

"It's twelve degrees out here!"

"I don't care. I'm going to have to pass this on to the boss. And he's not going to like it."

I make myself small. I try to stop breathing. I even close my eyes so they won't glow in a sweeping flashlight beam. And they run right by me! They actually miss the footprints and keep on going down the road. How lucky am I? So lucky! I mean, if you don't count the incredibly bad luck that landed me here in the first place, of course. I experience a surge of joy and happiness until I hear crunching in the snow right behind me. And my joy and happiness evaporate just like that.

"Did you really think you could run?" Suzie snarls.

I stay low. She comes closer.

"You left footprints," she says. "Your mother would be so proud."

I really don't like this Suzie. I shoot my leg out and hook her behind the ankles. Planting my arms in the snow for leverage, I snap my leg and she goes flying over backward. I didn't practice Snake in the Grass four thousand times for nothing. Suzie lands with a thud. The air rushes from her lungs.

"You are so dead," she groans.

I have a ten-second head start toward the lake before Suzie is back on her feet, gunning for me like a bee-stung bull. She closes the distance between us in no time.

"Just give up," she pants, right behind me. "That thing back there was pretty good, but it's probably all you've got, right? Where are you going to go anyway?"

I don't know, but I do know I won't stop until they catch me or I collapse. I pick up speed, the frosty air searing my lungs. And suddenly, there's a loud *crack* and the world under my feet shifts violently.

The water is up to my ankles before I realize we're on a patch of thin ice. A second later, the whole shelf collapses and both of us plunge into the freezing water.

I gasp as the water seeps quickly through my clothes. It's so cold my extremities go instantly numb. My jacket acts as an anchor and drags me under. I wrestle it off. On the other side of the gaping hole from where we fell in, the ice looks thicker. It might support my weight if I can get over there and pull myself out.

But Suzie has other ideas. She grabs me from behind, digging her fingers into my upper arms, and yanks me under.

"I can't swim, I can't swim," she shouts. I wrestle free

and spin toward her to find her eyes at full panic. Who doesn't know how to swim?

"Help me," she moans, and sinks beneath the surface. Now I panic. Sure, she's one of the bad guys, but I can't let her drown, can I? Doesn't that make me as bad as they are? I grab her by the back of the coat and, paddling frantically with one hand, pull us toward the thick ice ledge. By now I can't feel anything and my teeth chatter uncontrollably. Plus, I have no idea how to get the two of us out of here. I give Suzie a shake.

"Hey! Wake up!" I don't know if it's fear or she sucked down too much water, but Suzie is out cold. Which limits my options considerably. A bright light in my eyes distracts me from my efforts at not drowning. Tom.

"You shouldn't have run," he says. Is it the water in my ears, or has his voice gone suddenly much deeper? "It made me look bad."

"I wasn't really considering your feelings," I gasp.

"No," he says with all sincerity, "you weren't."

There's an important lesson here, and while I'm freezing to death, I think about it. Do not judge a book by its cover. Tom is cute and has nice eyes and a great smile, but none of that makes him a good person.

"Are you just going to stand there or what?" I ask.

I'm starting to feel faint, the round moon going all wavy. Suzie starts to slip from my grasp. "Your friend here is in trouble." Well, we're both in trouble, but at least I'm conscious. For the moment, anyway.

"I don't know what I'm going to do yet," Tom says.

"They're not going to like it if you let Suzie drown," I say, almost biting off my tongue. Tom shrugs. Suzie slips. My fingers are blue. Another minute in here and I'm a goner.

"She'll tell everyone I messed up," he says.

"No," I gurgle. "She'll owe you for saving her life. You'll be a hero." Tom furrows his brow. My vision narrows to a tunnel. "Hero."

Suzie wakes up with a start. "Tom," she gasps. "Get. Me. Out. Leave. The. Girl."

Wait a minute! I was saving your life! And I don't even like you! Without a word, Tom reaches down and takes Suzie by the scruff of the neck as if she's a newborn kitten. But as he goes to pull her out, I grab the sleeve of his jacket and haul him over into the water. He bellows with surprise. Scrambling, I use his body for leverage, propelling myself out of the water. I flop like a fish on the ice ledge and roll beyond Tom's grasp. Leave the girl? I think not.

"I can't believe I liked you!" Tom screams, clawing frantically at the ice. "I can't believe I thought you were pretty!"

Sure, Tom is awful and a liar and a traitor and an all-around terrible human being. But his compliment makes a nice little warm spot in my belly, now the only nonfrozen part of my anatomy. I stumble, hunched over, toward shore, slipping and sliding. My eyelashes freeze. My face burns. Up ahead, beams of light whip through the darkness like a Vegas laser show. As I draw closer, here's what I see.

Veronica. Beating the living daylights out of Rip Curl. What's he doing here? Why can't someone nice ever show up? I pause long enough to see Veronica's doing a pretty good job on him. He might be killing it at CrossFit, but that doesn't mean much in the real world, I guess. When Veronica spots me lurching toward them, she screams, "Abby, watch out!"

From out of the darkness, a soaking-wet Tom lunges at me and we hit the snow in a tangled heap.

"The Crow, Abby, the Crow!" The Crow? What's she screaming about? Oh right, that thing she showed me where you stick the pointy part of your elbow in your opponent's eye. Just like a crow pecking his dinner. "Now!"

I'm glad she can defend herself against Rip Curl and critique my performance at the same time. Tom pins me to the ground, grinning like a maniac. I jam my bent knee into his lower back. Ice cracks off my pants.

"Ow!" Tom bleats. In the split second he's distracted, I push him off me and deliver the Crow. He howls in pain, and I dash for the boat racks. Rip Curl has Veronica pushed up against the boathouse wall, his forearm across her neck, her feet five inches above the snow. He rants about how he's had enough of girls to last him a lifetime. Veronica struggles.

I dig into the nearest canoe and grab a wooden oar. Jennifer always says a girl needs to know how to do certain things, like hit a baseball, drive a stick shift, and rappel off a cliff. I swing that oar like nobody's business, and Rip Curl goes down.

Veronica gasps for air, clutching her throat. Behind me, Tom staggers to his feet, rubbing his eye. I give him a quick whack with the oar just to be on the safe side.

"Okay, Abby," Veronica says. "Stop hitting people now. Put that thing down."

But I don't want to put down my oar. I can't put it down. I'm suddenly light-headed and giddy.

"It's adrenaline," Veronica says softly, removing the oar from my hands and tossing it aside. "You're safe now. It's okay. Relax."

"Relax?" I squeak. "I don't think I can relax."

"That was nice work," she says, taking me by the hand and leading me back toward the road.

"I did Snake in the Grass and the Crow," I babble. "And the oar thing I just made up." There's a red mark across Veronica's throat. I start to cry.

"It's fine, Abby. This is a normal reaction. It's scary. You're okay now."

I don't know why I'm crying. I'm all jittery and my eyes dart this way and that, seeing danger in the shadows where there's nothing but trees. But in the moment, defending myself, I felt good. I felt powerful and able, and I didn't feel anything like the silly little girl I sometimes think the world sees when they look at me. But I also hurt those people. Sure, they were out to do me harm, but still—I hurt them. And I'm not sure that's supposed to feel good under any circumstances.

A white SUV appears out of the shadows. The lights glow warm and welcoming. Veronica puts her hands on my shoulders. "You did okay tonight," she says, "if we overlook all the parts where you screwed up." It's a sort of compliment. I spontaneously hug her. She goes stiff as a board. "What are you doing?" she says hotly.

"Nothing," I say, stepping back. "Sorry."

"Don't do that again. Spies don't hug."

"Spies don't hug," I repeat.

"And I didn't need saving back there," she huffs. "Just for the record, I had it totally under control."

Oh my God, I'm a real spy, and I saved Veronica's life even if she says I didn't! I stop before spontaneously hugging her again. She eyes me.

"What?" I ask.

"You are such a Lower Middle." But for the first time maybe ever, I finally see her smile. And here we are, grinning at each other, about to have the girl bonding moment of the century if I don't freeze to death first, when the front passenger door of the white SUV swings open and out steps Mrs. Smith.

Chapter 24

WHERE MRS. SMITH MAKES ME FEEL BAD. AGAIN.

"LADIES," MRS. SMITH SAYS, "Abigail is at risk of hypothermia. I suggest you get in the car."

The driver is a big man in a black suit wearing dark sunglasses even though it's the middle of the night. He doesn't acknowledge us as we climb in. My companions avert their eyes as I struggle into dry clothing and an enormous down parka while we fly down the icy road at an alarming speed. I wait patiently for Mrs. Smith to congratulate me for exceeding the expectations of a Lower Middle, but she doesn't say anything.

We drive in silence for about ten minutes, finally arriving at a single airstrip in seemingly the middle of nowhere.

A small prop plane sits on the tarmac, rotors spinning. The SUV brings us right up to the plane, kind of like we're royalty or the president or, you know, on television.

Mrs. Smith thanks the driver and we all pile out. The plane is tiny inside, a Coke can with wings, and we pitch and yaw all the way to the much-larger runways of San Francisco International. There, we transfer to a private jet. A private jet! Who are these people, anyway? But no one has said a word since we climbed into the SUV way back in the Sierra Nevada, so I don't ask. Only after we are settled into our comfortable leather seats does Mrs. Smith speak.

"I need to know everything that happened, Abigail," she says. "Every detail. Leave nothing out."

"But who were those people?" I blurt. "I think they work for Lotus Man and how did Rip Curl find me up there and who does he work for and—"

"That's none of your concern," she interrupts.

"But—"

"Remember, information is on a need-to-know basis. This is for your own safety."

"I don't care about my safety!" This comes out much louder than I expected. Mrs. Smith eyes me with pity as if I'm tragically miswired.

"Oh," she says smoothly, "but we do care. Very much. Now

walk me through the last twenty-four hours. All the details."

How come I don't exactly believe her level of concern for my welfare? We stare at each other until I understand that we can stare at each other for all eternity and she's still not going to tell me anything. I avert my eyes and jump in, starting my story at the airport with Fake Bronwyn and how she had everything right except the stumble with the password. "How would she have known all that?" I can't help but ask. "Is there someone on the inside, like a mole or a traitor or something?" Mrs. Smith frowns. She's about to remind me I don't need that information, that telling me anything will compromise my safety, but I cut her off. "Never mind," I say quickly, and continue with the story.

I plow through Tom and Rip Curl and the self-driving car and the snowy safe house and the triangle plaque and going out the window and running and finally ending up in the lake. Mrs. Smith does not look impressed. She does not congratulate me. She simply nods her head.

"I did not have the time to come out here and rescue you," she says. "I wish you'd followed directions." Her gaze moves to her phone.

"But—" I protest.

"You should get some rest," she says curtly.

"Why didn't Jennifer show up like she was supposed

to? Why didn't she come and get me? You said that was what was going to happen!"

Mrs. Smith's eyes dart back to me. "Clearly, I made an error in judgment," she says. "Now I have work to do." She slips on her reading glasses. I just failed Spying 101. But it's not fair! I did everything I was supposed to! She's the one who messed up. My eyes brim with hot tears. I fumble out of my seat belt and bolt for the lavatory at the back of the plane. It's one thing to cry. It's another thing to cry in front of Mrs. Smith.

I sit on the closed toilet and call Toby because there's no one else I can talk to about this. Toby pops up on the small screen and gives me a smile. I burst into tears.

"Oh hey, wait a minute," he says. "Are you okay?"

"No," I blubber. "I mean, yes, I am, but no, I'm not, you know?"

"Sure," he says quietly. "I get that."

"Mrs. Smith hates me," I whisper. "All I had to do was hang around and I couldn't get that right. And where was my mother? Why didn't she come?"

There's a pause while Toby shoves a handful of potato chips into his mouth. He's in his dorm room, at his desk, feet propped on his bed. He takes a swig of Coke. "I think the information Mrs. Smith had about Jennifer being in California was wrong."

"She said that?"

"No," Toby says. "I kind of overheard it. Sometimes they forget I'm in the room. Can you stop crying, please?"

"Okay," I sob, gushing more tears.

"Mrs. Smith got on the plane as soon as she realized what was happening. None of this is your fault."

It's nice of him to say so, but it doesn't change the way I feel, and the way I feel is surprisingly bad. I'm familiar with messing up. I did it all the time before I landed at Smith. But this feels different. I wanted to succeed. I wanted to show them that when it counted I could pull through. And I didn't.

"You didn't do anything wrong," Toby says.

"I should have known Bronwyn was Suzie," I say.

"How?"

"I don't know. Jennifer would have known."

"Don't do this to yourself, Abby."

Too late. "On the bright side"—I sniff—"your phone works after being submerged in freezing water."

"Really? Did you drop it in the sink?"

"Not exactly. I'll give you the details when I get back."

"I can't wait," he says with a smile.

"Thanks," I say. And I really mean it.

Chapter 25

WHERE TOBY CALLS ME NAMES.

THE NEXT NIGHT I'M BACK in the Annex with the crew, eating cheese fries as if nothing happened. Except Toby is being nice to me. As I lie my way through a story about a nonexistent wedding in San Francisco, Toby asks leading questions and fills in the bits that I leave out. But the girls are no dummies. Izumi looks from Toby to me and back to him.

"What's going on?" she asks bluntly. "Or maybe I don't want to know."

"What do you mean?" I ask.

"Oh, come on," Izumi says. "Really?"

"Really!" I say.

"You two, being nice to each other," Charlotte says. "It's weird."

"Yeah," says Quinn. He always takes Charlotte's side, no matter what. "Yeah, why are you being nice to her? You called her an annoying brat just, I don't know, like last week."

"An annoying brat?" I ask.

"He said you were, like, more annoying than one of those yappy dogs? What are they? Chihuahuas? Yeah. That's it. He called you an annoying Chihuahua. Always up in his business, you know?"

Toby punches him in the arm. "Shut up, man."

"What? You said it."

"God, you're an idiot. Abby, that's not what I meant."

I stand up. "Sure it is," I say, surprised at how much his comment stings. "I think I'm out of here."

Charlotte squeezes out from beside Quinn. "You are an idiot," she tells him. "And, Toby? You are too."

"Total idiot," Izumi concurs. "But are we surprised? Not really." We all tumble out of the Annex without looking back. The night air is biting cold, and we walk quickly back to McKinsey House.

"Don't let them bother you," Charlotte says.

"I won't," I say. "It doesn't."

"Yes, it does," Izumi says. "But who cares what Toby thinks, right?"

"Right," I agree.

And she has a point, an important one. I am still my own person despite what Toby or Mrs. Smith or Veronica think about me. I could have folded many times up there in the frozen mountains or running from Rip Curl, but I didn't. I kept at it even though I was scared. I'm like Jennifer that way. I don't quit. And everyone knows Jennifer was the best.

So maybe I didn't succeed in the way they wanted me to, but I'm still here. I'm still alive and upright, and I managed to get away. I'm suddenly proud of myself in a radically unfamiliar way. I do a little dance step and almost knock Charlotte over.

"What's with you?" she asks.

"Nothing." I grin. "Who cares what they think?"

"Yes!" Izumi cheers, pumping her fist in the air. "Wait—that's what I said."

"I know! And you're totally right!"

Izumi gives me a suspicious look. "I think you must have jet lag."

"Maybe," I say. "Hey, I gotta stop by and see Mrs. Smith real quick."

"Now?"

"Yeah, I was supposed to go earlier, but I kind of forgot."

"Okay," says Charlotte, "we'll see you back at the dorm."

I skip off in the direction of Mrs. Smith's office. I skip down Main Hall. Only when I'm about to round the corner do I pause. Mrs. Smith asked to see me, and I assume it's to tell me what happens next. But I'm done being bait. If Mrs. Smith wants my help, she's going to have to give me something in return.

And what I want is to be a superspy like my mother.

Chapter 26

WHERE I GET FIRED.

THROUGH THE SLIGHTLY ajar office doors, I hear Mrs. Smith on the phone. This all feels very familiar, except this time I have no intention of fainting.

"I had every right!" Mrs. Smith yells into the phone, pounding her fist on her desk. "Remember, it was a lapse in your intelligence that sent us on that wild-goose chase to California in the first place. You told me Jennifer was there. She wasn't! This stinks like a setup. We had a kite-surfing incident, for God's sake!"

There's a pause. Whoever is on the other end of the phone gives Mrs. Smith an earful. She holds the phone out about a foot and makes faces. How very unlike her! I suppress a giggle. I'm supposed to be here. She asked me to come and see her. But I still feel guilty, a shadow outside the door. Then again, pretending to be invisible is how Toby gets all his good information.

"Yes, plan B, of course," Mrs. Smith says softly into the phone. "And no, the girl isn't part of that plan. Yes, that's a promise. Listen, we just have to think like Jennifer, do what she would do, and we'll find her and the evidence."

Another pause. I swear I can see steam billowing from Mrs. Smith's ears. She's about to lose her cool, something I've never seen and would not have thought possible. "I understand no one thinks like Jennifer and that's why she's the best!" she shouts. "You don't think I know that? Good God, my entire life has been spent trying to understand that woman!"

I pick this moment to push the office door open, making as much noise as possible. If I was confident about asking for what I want five seconds ago, I'm less so now.

"I have to go," Mrs. Smith says quickly when she sees me. She slams down the receiver without bothering to say good-bye. She straightens her suit jacket, rearranges some pens on her desk, and offers me an unconvincing smile.

"Abigail," she says. "Come in."

"You wanted to see me?"

"Sit down, please." She gestures toward a seat in front of her desk. I sit and try not to fidget. It's not easy.

"Listen," I begin. "I know it didn't go so well out in California, but I think I did okay not drowning and escaping the house and . . ."

Mrs. Smith holds up a manicured hand. I stop speaking. "Things are complicated, Abigail. As such, we've decided to take a different approach to resolving this situation, one that no longer requires your assistance. You're free to resume your normal activities."

Hold up. Did I just get fired? "It's been a long-standing rule of the Smith School not to involve children under the age of sixteen in this sort of work," Mrs. Smith continues. "We walk a fine line with those who pay the bills. There are some who believe our tactics are morally question-able. These people wait for us to make a mistake. Natu-rally, I take full responsibility for this operation's failure." She grimaces. She might take responsibility, but she's not enjoying it. The bits of the conversation I overheard fall into place. She was talking about how plan B doesn't include me.

"But wait," I blurt. "I want to be a spy!"

It's true that mere days ago, I found the whole idea of teenage-girl spies preposterous. But now that I'm being kicked out of the club, I'm suddenly desperate to stay.

"Excuse me?"

"I want to be one of you! I want to be terrifying like Veronica and smart, and I don't ever want to be sitting there on a pier like that, all innocent, ever again. I want to be good at this. Like my mom."

Mrs. Smith rubs her eyes. She looks pale and tired as if the weight of the world sits on her shoulders. Plus, I think I'm giving her a headache.

"This isn't the time, Abigail," she says.

"But I don't want to wait until I'm sixteen. I want to do it now."

"It's forbidden."

"Well, it wasn't yesterday," I point out. "Yesterday I was in on it."

"That was different."

"How?"

"We were using you," she replies bluntly. "We thought we had a shortcut to what we wanted. We didn't."

Although she claims responsibility, her tone places the blame for this current disaster squarely on my shoulders. Had I not gone off with the fake Bronwyn, had I not gotten snatched off the pier or gone joyriding in the Headless Prius, none of this would have happened. My cheeks grow hot.

Mrs. Smith sighs. "We tested you, Abigail," she says, "as we test all our incoming students. And you have no inherent aptitude for this type of work. So it's probably best if we just forget this whole episode and move on. You'll have a very rewarding experience here at Smith and go on to do many great things with your life." She stands. "And don't worry about your mother. We have it well in hand."

Is she insane? I'm supposed to just go back to life as it was before I discovered that a) this place is a secret breeding ground for spies, and b) my mother is one of them? No way. A girl can forget a lot of things, but that is asking too much.

"But I—"

"I'm afraid my decision is final."

Before I can pitch a true hissy fit (I can do a pretty good one when motivated), there's a knock at the door and Mr. Roberts appears.

"Can I see you for a moment?" he asks Mrs. Smith. "Oh hello, Abigail. How was the wedding?"

"It was nice, sir," I say.

"Well, I'm very pleased to hear that," he says. "Headmaster?"

"Now?" Mrs. Smith asks.

"Yes, now," Mr. Roberts says. Boy, Mrs. Smith is not having the best night. She sighs but gets up and follows

Mr. Roberts into the hallway, closing the door behind her, leaving me alone in her office. The way I see it, I have two options. I can press my ear to the door and eavesdrop, or I can snoop through the papers on Mrs. Smith's desk. I choose the desk.

And this is where I find the same pencil sketch of the statue I saw the last time I snooped around on Mrs. Smith's desk. What's it still doing here? Does it mean something? It's too random not to mean anything. It has to be a clue. As the office door starts to open, I stuff it in my pocket and slap a happy grin on my face. But my effort is wasted. Mrs. Smith looks so distracted I could be on fire and she wouldn't notice me.

"So can I go now?" I ask. "It's going to be lights-out soon."

Mrs. Smith waves me away with a "Good evening, Miss Hunter," and I slip out without a word. As I make my way down Main Hall and past the dining hall, I have the spark of an idea. As I pass the senior student lounge and the stairway down to the Stern Music Wing, the idea grows legs. Out the door and across the quad toward McKinsey House, the idea calcifies into a plan.

The reason Mrs. Smith and Jennifer worked so well together was because they knew each other better than anyone else. It was the basis of their communication, things no one else would understand. But this time Mrs. Smith couldn't figure out what Jennifer meant by the clue I now have stuffed in my pocket. But I can. Despite everything I've been told over the last few days about my mother, I still know her better than anyone. I'm going to prove to Mrs. Smith, Veronica, and everyone else that I'm more than I appear. I'm going to show them that firing me was a terrible mistake. If something needs finding, I'm just the girl to do it.

Chapter 27

WHERE I LEARN YOU CAN'T PULL A FAST ONE ON YOUR FRIENDS.

BY THE TIME I CLIMB to the fourth floor of McKinsey House, I'm downright giddy with the idea of taking action. But when I see Charlotte and Izumi waiting for me in my room, my resolve falters. They look serious. They look like they're prepared for an intervention. I pause. Charlotte sticks her head out into the hallway.

"We see you," she says. I could run, but that would be obvious.

"Hi," I say casually. "What's up?" The bell rings for lights-out. The girls don't budge.

"Why don't you tell us?" Izumi asks. She sounds just like a mom. It's terrifying.

"What do you mean?"

Izumi snorts. Charlotte rolls her eyes. "Come on, Abby," she says. "You've been acting weird. Don't deny it. You keep disappearing and you're tired all the time and that going to California in the middle of the week and missing the Chinese History exam? Who does that?"

"Is it a boy? Are you sick?" Izumi asks.

"Or tutoring? Or did you, like, join the band and are too embarrassed to tell us?" Charlotte adds.

They warned me in no uncertain terms that everything Center-related was to be kept secret. I was not to tell anyone anything.

But you know what? They fired me.

"You guys are not going to believe this," I say. They move closer, eyes wide with expectation. "But you'd better sit down."

I start at the beginning with Lotus Man on the bus. They interrupt only to ask how tall Tom was and what color eyes he had and if I got his cell number. I finish with my idea about finding Jennifer. What follows is complete silence. I could hear the crickets if they weren't all frozen for the winter. For the first time, my friends appear speechless.

Finally, Izumi asks, "Are you crazy? I mean, like, for-real crazy?"

"No."

"Okay," she says. "I had to ask."

"I know," I say.

"This is so. Messed. Up," Charlotte says, her eyes blazing. "I knew Jennifer was cool, and not parent cool, you know? How awesome! And Veronica! I'm having a problem with Toby, though."

"He does always knows things before anyone else," Izumi says. "Can you sneak me down to the catacombs? I have got to see some of his toys." She's practically drooling.

"No," I say, but hand her the iPhone as a consolation prize. "Don't play Solitaire."

"Why?"

"It blows up."

"Glitchy?"

"You might say that."

"So what do we do?" Charlotte asks.

"Do?"

"Yeah. You said you were going to find whatever Jennifer hid. How does that work?"

I pull the crumbled clue from my pocket and smooth it flat on my thigh. "By figuring out what this means," I say.

"What is it?" Izumi says.

"I don't know," I say.

"So how does that help us?" asks Charlotte.

"Us?"

"Yeah, us."

"No way," I say.

"Yes way," says Izumi.

"You can't come with me. You'll get busted."

"So what?" Charlotte says.

"Listen," Izumi says, "my dad just donated five million dollars for the new science center. They won't kick me out." Okay. Hard to argue with that one, but still.

"It's too dangerous," I say. For some reason this cracks them up. "I'm not kidding!"

"If you can do it, we can," Charlotte declares.

How do I explain to them how scared I was when Rip Curl grabbed me? Or how I really thought it was over in that frozen lake? Or how it feels to be used and discarded? I can't. This is something you have to learn for yourself.

"You'll blame me when things turn ugly," I say, "and they will turn ugly, no doubt."

"We won't," Charlotte promises. "We swear. We'll do a blood-sisters thing if you want."

"That's gross," says Izumi. I eye my friends, a lump rising in my throat.

"You guys really want to come with me?"

"Yes," Charlotte and Izumi say in unison. "So what's the plan?"

Before I can explain I have a plan but no real idea about how to execute it, there's a commotion outside my window. I rush to raise it only to find Toby, sweaty and out of breath, clinging to the window ledge like an amateur Spider-Man.

"What are you doing?" I shriek. "You could fall!" Charlotte and I each grab an arm and haul him over the edge. He tumbles to the floor in a haphazard heap and doesn't move until Charlotte nudges him with her toe.

"Are you okay?" she asks.

"No," he groans. "That was not cool. I'm never doing that again."

"Why'd you do it in the first place?" I ask.

"It's after lights-out and I had to talk to you," he says, untangling and sitting up.

"You could have texted," Izumi suggests.

"Nope," Toby says. "This had to be done face-to-face." He clears his throat as if preparing to give a speech. He wipes his palms on his pants. "Okay. So I'm really sorry for the things I said about you to Quinn."

"So you admit you said them?" Charlotte asks.

Toby looks sheepish. "Yes. But I didn't mean any of it. You aren't annoying, Abby. You're not."

"You called her an annoying Chihuahua," Izumi reminds him. Toby glares at her.

"Thanks for that," he mutters. "Abby, I'm sorry."

"Great," says Charlotte. "Thanks for coming. Good-bye, now. Please take the stairs." She shoves him toward the door. Toby looks at me beseechingly. I look away. I'm not done being insulted yet. Charlotte and Izumi push him the rest of the way out the door. "You need to go. We're busy. Places to go, people to find."

"Wait," says Toby. "What did you say?" He finally sees the iPhone in Izumi's hands. His eyes dart to me. "Tell me you didn't."

I shrug. "Mrs. Smith fired me," I say.

"Oh, Abby." He looks upset. "And you think you're just going to slide on out of here and find Jennifer Hunter?" I nod. "You aren't a spy! You were never meant to be a spy!"

"No one knows Jennifer better than I do," I retort, getting angry. "You think you do, with your stories and pictures, but you're wrong. I can find whatever she's hidden. And that's exactly what I intend to do."

"What *we* intend to do," Charlotte corrects me.

"Right. We."

Toby plants his feet like I'm going to sweep them out from under him (which I can do now) and crosses his arms. "No way."

"Just try and stop us," Izumi challenges.

"I'm coming with you," he says flatly.

"You're not invited," Charlotte replies.

"If you go without me, I'll go right to Mrs. Smith and you won't get past Main Gate before you get busted."

"Are you blackmailing us?" I ask.

"Sort of," he says with a smile.

"Why?" Why does he want to join in on this? Our chances of complete failure are pretty high.

"Because blackmail works."

"No, not that. Why do you want to come?"

Toby scans the room, clearly deciding if this is something he wants to say in front of all of us. He sighs. "If I want to go to the strategy school in Florida," he says, "I have to show some real-world experience. I have to get out of here. "

"Real-world experience?" asks Izumi. "For an application

to a school that's supposed to teach you that? That's totally twisted."

"You're only a Middle," Charlotte points out. "Isn't it a little soon?"

"Are you kidding me?" Toby asks. "Do you know how competitive it is out there? Some kids will do anything to get a leg up."

"Like get busted and kicked out of Smith?" Izumi asks.

Toby glares. "It's showing initiative. That's application gold."

I, for one, cannot believe we're having this conversation. Ultimately, if I turn Toby down, we don't get out of here. If I say yes, well, then we're saddled with him.

"Fine," I say. "Under one condition. And you have to be honest or we're leaving you here."

Toby stiffens. "Okay," he says slowly.

"That Veronica creature I saw on the wall of Mrs. Smith's office . . . Why did you do that to me?"

Toby raises both his hands in immediate defense. "It was just a new spyware thing I was trying to get to work. I call it Spy Eye and it's pretty cool. You project an image into a room over preexisting security cameras and the image itself acts as a recording device, letting you see way more than you can with just the camera, like every-square-inch kind of thing. I could see you under the couch. I positioned the image for your eyes only. It's better than hacking the actual security system, but the sound doesn't work right, so you could hear me but I couldn't hear you. It was nothing personal. I swear. I don't know what I was thinking."

This sounds like the truth. I decide to accept his apology and let him get thrown out of school along with the rest of us. "Go get your stuff and meet us by the west stone wall in fifteen minutes," I say. "If you're not there, we leave without you. And don't get caught, okay? And watch out for Betty and Barney!"

But Toby is already gone.

Chapter 28

ESCAPE FROM THE SMITH SCHOOL FOR CHILDREN. AGAIN.

AFTER TOBY LEAVES, WE SPLIT UP, fill our backpacks with things we think we'll need, and regroup in my room. "So what's the plan?" Charlotte asks, adding my hairbrush to her bag.

"We figure out this clue," I say, "and go from there."

"What does it mean?"

"Well, it could be a lot of things—" I say.

"She has no idea," interrupts Izumi.

"This was a short-lived adventure," Charlotte says, throwing up her hands. "We don't even have a step one."

"Now, wait a minute," says Izumi. "Let's think this

through. Abby knows Jennifer better than these other people do, right?"

"Yes." That's what I've been telling myself, anyway, but really, how well do I know her if she's been living a double life right in front of me and I had no idea?

"So if you were her, where would you hide something important that you didn't want found?"

That's easy. "New York City," I say. Every time we stepped outside our apartment, my mother would take a deep inhale of stinky exhaust-poisoned air and say, 'No place to get lost like New York.' Of course, New York City is four hundred and sixty-nine square miles in size with a population of eight and one-half million and I'm just going on a hunch.

"So that's step one," says Charlotte. "We go to New York City."

"And by the time we get there, we'd better have figured out what that clue means," Izumi adds. My stomach does an uncomfortable flip-flop. What am I getting us into?

Ten minutes later we slip out of McKinsey House undetected. There's no need for us to go out a window because I have the code. We wait until Betty and Barney pass with the night security guard and sprint for the west stone wall, where Toby waits for us. He's nervous, jumping from foot to foot and rubbing his cold hands.

"Turn off your cell phones," he whispers.

"Why?"

He rolls his eyes. "Because if you don't, they can follow us."

I don't ask who "they" are. I turn off my phone.

We board the same bus, but this time we make it to the Stamford train station without interference. We catch our train and settle in. We're a strange little group, but the train is practically empty, so we go undetected.

We sit two across, facing each other, leaning in, heads together, and brainstorm ways to find my mother. At least, that's what I thought would happen.

Here's how it really goes:

"I'm hungry," whines Toby.

"This train smells like pee," Charlotte complains.

"Oh my God, I forgot my Chinese History book!" says Izumi.

"Can you guys stop whining?" I ask.

"Don't be so bossy," Charlotte says.

"I'm not being bossy!" I yell.

"We don't use the word 'bossy' to describe girls anymore," Izumi says. "It's condescending. If a boy acts in the same way, he's called a leader. And people are staring."

"No, they're not," I say.

"Hey, Toby?" Charlotte says.

"Yeah?"

"Can't you get Quinn to, like, stop following me around? It's creepy."

"You might as well ask me to go to Mars."

"You'll be able to go to Mars in probably twenty years," says Izumi.

"Can you guys please focus?" I beg. "We're going to be there soon, and we have no idea what the clue means."

"Maybe Jennifer will just find us and we can ask her?" Charlotte says.

Toby shakes his head. "No way."

"Why not?"

"Because no one knows we're doing this."

"I'm not sure that matters," I say.

"Let's just say I planted a few bits of evidence before I left that aren't actually true."

"You what?"

"Misled some people so we could get a head start."

Izumi hums the Darth Vader theme from *Star Wars*. Toby punches her in the arm. We crack up, practically falling out of our seats. It's not that funny. We're just all tired and freaked out.

"Okay, okay," I say. "Enough. We still have no idea where to begin looking."

"I really don't like Quinn," says Charlotte.

"That's obvious," says Toby.

"He's a little needy," adds Izumi.

"Hey," I say. "How about we direct some energy toward a problem that matters?"

"Jeez, what's she so worked up over?" says Charlotte.

"Delusions of grandeur," says Toby. "She thinks she's a spy and we're her minions. I've seen this happen before."

"I do not think you're my minions!" I protest.

"You're awfully sensitive," says Izumi.

"I am not!"

"Quit shouting," says Toby. "People are looking."

I spend the next ten minutes sulking. That my friends hardly notice does not improve my mood. I should have left them at school. Finally, our train pulls into Grand Central Terminal, which at this hour smells deliciously like bagels and croissants. Toby has to stop for sustenance lest he keel over dead from calorie deprivation. "I'm a thirteen-year-old boy," he grouses. "I eat. It's what we do."

We veer left from where our track exits into the terminal and head toward Zaro's. On the way, I take a moment to gaze at the constellations on the ceiling. This is one of my favorite places. Jennifer and I once came here on a Sunday morning when the terminal was empty, except for a few stragglers, and lay on the floor for a perfect ceiling view. Yes, lying on the floor of a train station that services roughly 750,000 passengers per day is kind of gross, but Jennifer said the experience made it worth the risk. "Sometimes you have to see the bigger picture," she said.

"Hey, snap out of it." Charlotte yanks me back to reality. We are at the front of the Zaro's line, and if we don't order promptly, we will be set upon by a horde of angry commuters. This is not the place to daydream.

Toby buys two bagels with cream cheese and a hot chocolate. Charlotte, Izumi, and I split a black-and-white cookie, a doughnut, and a Diet Coke. These are not healthy choices, but neither is running away from boarding school.

Breakfast in hand, we head to the lower concourse and find an empty table in a corner. A good spy sits with her back to the wall so she can see the whole room. That's not a Veronica-ism, in case you're wondering. I think I read it in a book. I lay the pencil sketch on the table.

"So Jennifer's a world-class doodler," I explain. "It's like she has to have her hands moving all the time. Have you guys noticed how Mrs. Smith paces?" I get nods all around. "Well, this is just Jennifer's version of pacing."

"And?" Charlotte prompts.

"I took this from Mrs. Smith's desk," I continue. "It has to be the clue she couldn't figure out."

"Did they take it from your house?" Izumi asks.

"No," says Toby. This is exactly the way he usually reveals gossip that no one could possibly know: His voice drops an octave and goes quiet, making us lean in to hear. "It came from a pizza place."

"Jake's!" I shout, leaping from my seat and nearly upending the table. "The place on the corner! Jennifer always hangs her sketches on the giant bulletin boards there." Blank looks from my friends. "Jake's an amateur artist," I explain. "He likes to give other amateur artists a chance to publicly display their art. He calls the wall the 'artists' corner.' It's just a pizza place, but I guess it works for some people."

Izumi drums her fingers on the table, her brow furrowed. Charlotte elbows her. "Spill it," she says.

"I'm just thinking," she says.

"You're always doing that," Charlotte says.

"Someone has to. Anyway, Jennifer takes her little pictures and puts them on the bulletin board, right?"

"Yes."

"Are the pictures the same every time?"

"No. They're totally random, actually. Why?"

Izumi takes the sketch and holds it right up to her nose. She turns it upside down and sideways.

"What are you doing?" asks Charlotte.

"See how the page has creases all over it?" she says. She puts the sketch back on the table and begins to bend it this way and that along the preexisting folds. We watch, holding our breath.

"Aha!" she yelps, holding up the sketch. She's folded it in half lengthwise and then again in a series of triangles as if making a paper fan. "Look." Where the folds meet, there are nine neat symbols—an arrow; a star; the symbols for Aries, Leo, and Gemini; the infinity symbol; a cracked heart; something that looks like the Liberty Bell; and finally, a cross.

"This can't be a coincidence," Izumi whispers.

"There are no coincidences," I add. "Coincidences stink."

"I totally agree," says Charlotte. "But what do they mean?"

Everyone looks at me. "I have no idea." The atmosphere around us deflates. "But maybe we need to go to Jake's and ask him what he knows? Maybe he's in on it? I mean, she's been passing messages off at his place for as long as I can remember."

"Why so Luddite, though?" asks Charlotte. "Why not, you know, text or something? It's faster."

"Duh," Toby says. "Electronic footprint? Nothing in cyberspace is secure. I love technology, but not when you're trying to fly below the radar. Teflon's got it right on that one. Hey, Charlotte?"

"What?"

"Will you go get me a chocolate croissant?"

"You're kidding, right?"

"How about a slice of pizza?" I say. "Let's go see Jake."

We collect our stuff and head out of Grand Central into a sunny but cold New York City morning.

Chapter 29

WHERE I REALIZE WHAT IS RIGHT IN FRONT OF MY FACE.

JAKE'S PIZZA IS A TINY DIVE around the corner from our apartment, with an inch of grease on the windows and five mismatched tables. It's always one thousand degrees inside regardless of the season because of the giant pizza oven, which, according to Jake, came from an old Italian villa and was shipped here in one piece. There are windows facing the sidewalk and a wall covered entirely in corkboard. This is the artists' corner, and the board is plastered in paintings and comics and sketches and poems and photographs and collage. There's even a small table for sculpture if you're brave enough to leave one.

Jake's is a fine place and the pizza's good, don't get me

wrong, but I always thought Jennifer liked it way more than seemed reasonable. When I was little, we used to go there a lot, and she always had something to add to the wall. She'd laugh as she pinned up whatever doodle had jumped from her brain onto the paper as if it were all so innocent. But now I see it's not. Now I see this was Jennifer's supersecret communication method. Untraceable. Totally secure. Meaningless to almost everyone.

We arrive at the corner of Eleventh Street and Second Avenue only to find Jake's Pizza closed. Of course, it's not even eight thirty in the morning, and according to the sign in the window, the shop doesn't open until noon. We sit down on the steps of the apartment building next door. This is not an auspicious beginning to our sleuthing. But being as I'm the de facto team leader, I feel obligated to keep up our spirits.

"This isn't a big deal," I say. "We can wait." Charlotte gives me an incredulous look.

"Are you kidding me?" she complains. "It's freezing. Let's go to Starbucks and have hot chocolate."

"We're low on funds," I remind her.

"So what?" She shrugs. "I have Daddy's emergencies-only credit card committed to memory."

"Did you not hear what I said about the electronic

footprint?" Toby says. "Why don't you just broadcast our whereabouts to the entire world? No credit cards. No phones."

But I see Charlotte's point. My fingers are freezing, and I bet Starbucks is toasty warm. Plus, they have those miniscones I really like. When I'm just about to concede that taking the risk of stealing Charlotte's dad's credit card is worth it, Jake emerges from the apartment building behind us. He wears pj bottoms with aliens on them, a stained white T-shirt, and pink bunny slippers. He scratches his large, doughy belly and yawns.

"Hey, Abby," he says, as if finding me outside his front door is not even a little weird. "You guys don't happen to have any coffee, do you? I could really use some."

We shake our heads. Toby holds out a scrap of bagel wrapped in paper. With a nod of thanks, Jake takes it.

"Jake, these are my friends Charlotte, Toby, and Izumi," I say.

"And you're out here on my steps because why?" he says with his mouth full. "It's not lunchtime yet, is it? If you want slices, I gotta get the oven going and things. Might be a little while."

"No," I say. "We're actually wondering about this." I pull out the sketch and hold it up for him to see. He smiles.

"One of Mrs. Hunter's," he says. He always refers to her as Mrs. Hunter, even though she's told him a thousand times she's not a missus and he should call her Jennifer.

"Was it up on your wall?" I ask. "Did Jennifer put it up there?"

"You mean your mother?" he asks. "Does she know you call her Jennifer?"

I hang my head. "Did my mom bring it in?"

Jake takes the sketch and studies it close. "Yeah," he says finally, "probably last week sometime. I remember because she seemed all tired and twitchy. You know how people get when they're nervous? Well, that was Jennifer all right. Her eyes were bouncing around like electricity."

"And?" Charlotte prompts.

"She had a slice," he continues. "She always says nice things about my pizza. She's a great lady, your mom. After she left, I thought I should have asked after her, you know? Being a single mom in New York City is no easy thing." I experience an unexpected wave of guilt thinking of all Jennifer's text messages, about what she's having for lunch or who she ran into at the gym or what she's reading, that I don't even bother to read.

"Did you by any chance notice who took the sketch from the board?" Izumi asks politely.

"Yup," he says immediately. "She was a tiny thing, wearing high heels. Blond hair. Never saw her before. Kind of scary."

"Mrs. Smith," we say in unison.

"Whoever," Jake says with a shrug. "It's part of the deal when you put stuff up. A person likes something, she takes it. It's the big circle of art, you know?"

We nod like it makes perfect sense.

Jake gets to his feet, rubs his eyes, and stretches. "Okay," he says. "You guys have fun doing whatever it is you're doing and be safe. Come back later if you want a slice. I'm going for coffee." In bunny slippers and his pj's, Jake heads down the street to Starbucks. We watch him go with equal parts awe and dismay.

Ten minutes later, we sit on a park bench in Union Square. It's cold, so we mostly have the park to ourselves.

"Do you think that message was intended for Mrs. Smith?" Charlotte asks. "Or was it more like an interception?"

"Well, this is how Jennifer and Mrs. Smith worked back in the old days," says Toby. "Jennifer got the intelligence or whatever, left the clues, and then ran interference while Mrs. Smith swooped in and picked up whatever Jennifer left for her. I bet Jennifer was counting on Mrs. Smith being able to do it again, like before."

"But this time Mrs. Smith didn't understand the clue and couldn't find what Jennifer left for her," Izumi says. "And so she figured she'd shortcut her way using Abby."

"Which was an epic fail," Toby says.

"Where is Jennifer anyway?" Charlotte asks.

"We're totally in stealth mode," Toby reminds her. "Even Teflon would have a hard time tracking us."

"So what do we do now?" asks Charlotte.

I dig out the sketch and examine the symbols. They still mean nothing to me. I unfold the paper and smooth it out.

Izumi sniffles. "Are you okay?" I ask.

"I hate the idea we won't always be friends," she says softly. "Like Jennifer and Mrs. Smith."

"You don't know that," Charlotte says. "Maybe we should do the blood-sisters thing?"

Toby snorts. "The Persephone Club girls did that," he says. "Look how well it worked out for them."

"Persephone Club?" Charlotte asks, confused.

As Toby explains about the founding spy school class, the name Persephone rattles around in my brain, looking to lock on. According to Greek mythology, Persephone, daughter of Demeter, was kidnapped by Hades and forced to live six months of every year in the Underworld. Demeter, goddess of the harvest, mourned her daughter's absence during these months and let everything on earth die. This was the way the ancient Greeks explained the changing seasons. But why does it matter?

"Persephone," I mutter. "Persephone." The word continues to bang around until finally it stops. I gasp.

"What?" Toby asks.

"Persephone!" I yell, holding up the sketch. "This is the statue of Persephone at the Frick! The one in the courtyard."

"Huh?"

"It's the bronze Persephone at the Frick museum," I say. "In the Garden Court? I've been there with Jennifer a million times. It's one of her favorite FFF destinations."

"Stop speaking in code," says Toby.

"Forced Family Fun," I say. "It's when Jennifer makes us do stuff together that I don't want to do."

"Interesting," says Toby.

"Not really," I say.

"But what about the symbols?" Izumi asks.

"I still have no idea about the symbols, but the statue is a definite."

"So where is this Frack place, anyway?" Charlotte asks.

"The Frick. Seventieth Street," I say. "Near Central Park."

"We better go have a look," Toby says.

We start walking. The complaining starts almost immediately. Charlotte's feet hurt. Toby wants snacks. Izumi is cold.

"Quit whining," I say. "Keep walking."

"Can't we take a cab?" Charlotte asks.

"After Zaro's, we don't have much money left," I say. At school, no one really needs cash when they are on campus, so we didn't start this little adventure with much to begin with. And Toby's no-credit-card rule. Everyone pulls out their change and crumpled bills and piles them into Izumi's hands.

She counts. "Eight dollars and thirty-seven cents."

"No cab," I say.

"I'll pay," Charlotte says. She holds up her phone, the Uber app filling the small screen.

"No!" Toby yells. "Turn it off!"

"Relax!" Charlotte yells back. "Besides, it's too late. I already requested a car."

Toby grabs the phone from her. His thumbs fly. "I told you no phones," he hisses.

"You need to just chill out," Charlotte hisses back. Toby powers down the phone and throws it back to her. Izumi looks at me, wide-eyed.

"It was only a minute," I say in Charlotte's defense. "Probably no big deal."

"You're so naive," Toby snaps. "It only takes a minute for people like that to track us."

It reminds me of why Veronica called me "innocent," and I can't argue because he's right. Before my friends move on to beating each other up, an Uber car pulls up curbside. You can't spit in New York City without hitting an Uber car, but Jennifer never lets us use them. She says she doesn't like having her every move tracked. Cash and the bus, she always says. I thought she was just being old-school and stubborn, but probably it was more than that.

"Yay!" Charlotte says, pulling open the rear passenger door. The driver window is shaded, so I can't see who's behind the wheel, and just recently I've developed a phobia of driverless vehicles.

"Wait!" I yell. "We don't know anything about this car!"

"Abby," says Izumi, "it's Uber. Its job is to take us places. You need to relax." Izumi hops in beside Charlotte. We may have had a breach in our stealth mode, but the car is appealing nonetheless.

"It is kind of cold out here," Toby mumbles. He slides in next. I don't feel good about this. I feel the same tingling I did in the airport with Fake Bronwyn, but maybe I'm crazy? My friends seem to think this is just fine. Probably Izumi is right and I need to relax. Maybe we all do.

Chapter 30

WHERE WE FIND OUT SOMETHING INTERESTING ABOUT TOBY.

WE ARRIVE AT THE MUSEUM, warm and comfortable. There have been no complaints for at least fifteen minutes, which is a record so far. The Frick Collection is housed in what used to be the personal residence of Henry Clay Frick, a steel magnate in the early 1900s. Being very rich, he set about building himself a mini Palace of Versailles right next to Central Park. The apartment I share with Jennifer is nine hundred square feet, so it is hard to imagine having enough space to play regulation basketball in the living room. Eventually, the mansion and the art collection were turned into the museum upon whose steps we now stand. But eight dollars and thirty-seven cents is not going to be enough to get us in the door.

I cautiously approach the lady behind the ticket desk. She wears a navy-blue cardigan covered in cat hair and a name tag that identifies her as Gladys. Her lips form a tight line, suggesting she is not excited by what I'm going to say even if I haven't said it yet.

"My dear," Gladys says, "we really do prefer children be accompanied by adults. It's a rule, and we have it for a reason."

"I'm a member," I blurt out. "We're writing a paper on Vermeer versus Rembrandt and we'll fail unless we get in to see the paintings."

"And this is my problem how exactly?" she asks, her eyes drifting back to the *New York Times* open on her desk. Charlotte appears beside me and hip-checks me out of the way.

"Ma'am," Charlotte says with a smile, "that color blue really brings out the violet in your eyes. They're stunning. Did you model?"

What is she doing? She's going to get us pitched out of here in a hot minute. But something in Gladys's face softens. She runs a hand down the arm of her own sweater as if noticing it for the first time.

"Is it cashmere?" Charlotte continues. "It looks so soft. Makes me want to pet you like a cat." She giggles. Certainly now she's gone too far? But no, Gladys actually smiles and giggles right along with Charlotte.

"I got it at Goodwill," Gladys says. "It was a steal! People don't know a good thing when they see it."

"I know," Charlotte says. "But I could tell right away you have a keen eye. It's probably why you're such a valuable member of the museum team, right? I bet you know this stuff inside and out. We can only hope to attain your level of knowledge."

"What is she doing?" Izumi whispers in my ear.

"Getting us into the museum," I whisper back.

"Amazing," Izumi says in awe.

"No kidding."

Gladys puts down her paper and grins at Charlotte. "I don't want you kids to fail," she says, suddenly a vision of concern for our academic futures. "What is this paper on?"

We don't take Art History until we're Upper Middles, but I've listened to the museum's audio tour about seven hundred times and just hope I can come up with something. I clear my throat and step forward. But Charlotte beats me to it.

"We're examining how while Rembrandt reached for grandeur, Vermeer favored quieter, more ordinary scenes," she says with a shy smile. "We need to explain how this affects the experience of each artist's work, and in order to explain the experience we need to get in here and, you know, experience the art."

We are so in.

After a pause, Gladys says, "An impressive thesis for a young person. I'm inclined to let you in if you promise to behave. Now, did one of you mention being a member?"

"And that's how it's done," Charlotte whispers as we thank Gladys and race into the museum before she changes her mind.

Once inside, I head right for the Garden Court. The morning light filters through the glass-paneled ceiling, bathing the space in a calming yellow glow. I immediately feel better. I don't know why, but I do.

In the middle of the long, rectangular courtyard is an oblong pond with a fountain at one end. Opposite the fountain is a bench. We sit on the bench.

"Now what?" Charlotte whispers. There at the other end near the fountain is the statue of Persephone from the drawing. I have sat on this very bench with Jennifer a hundred times and yet it took me days to figure out what I was looking at on the paper. What else am I missing?

I get the feeling this is like Jake's. We go there all the time not because the pizza is good but because Jennifer uses the board to communicate. So if we come here all the time, it's probably not because Jennifer really likes the art. She has to be using this space for something too.

"Abby?" says Toby.

"Yeah?"

"Look." He points to the far side of the very large room to a sign indicating the direction of the restrooms.

"You don't have to ask permission. Just go."

"You're hilarious. Look at the symbol. The arrow. It's the first one of the nine. On the paper."

"Like I Spy!" Charlotte shouts.

"Of course," says Izumi. "Why didn't I think of that? We find the symbols in sequence and that leads us to the prize. Whatever that is."

I love my friends. They are proving to be just the sort of accomplices an aspiring spy girl like me needs. "Jennifer does make me play I Spy more than is normal."

Quickly, I refold the paper so we can see all nine symbols. We jump off the bench and huddle by the arrow on the wall. "The star is next," I say. Slowly, we spin in circles, looking everywhere for a star. Izumi finds one in a painting in the Oval Room, and we dash in that direction. A guard glares at us and we slow down. The Frick is a small museum by New York standards; only a handful of rooms.

We need to be careful lest we get thrown out for acting like lunatics and break Gladys's heart.

We stand in front of the painting and spin again. This time Charlotte finds a small sculpture of the Aries ram. We go on like this for a good forty-five minutes before reaching the last item on the list, the cross. It doesn't take long to find a marble statue of a warrior holding a sword and a cross.

"Is this the evidence?" Charlotte asks, circling the artwork.

Toby shakes his head. "No, but I think Abby's right. It's close."

"It's under the statue," says Izumi with confidence.

"How do you know?"

"I don't, but where else is it going to be?"

"It wouldn't fit under the statue," I say. "Plus, it's alarmed. We can't touch it."

"What if it's a tiny piece of microfilm?" Izumi asks.

"Or one of those miniature scrolls you can only read with a magnifying glass?" adds Toby.

"Hey, guys," Charlotte says. The plaque identifying the statue and its artist is mounted on the pedestal in such a way that it protrudes about an inch. Charlotte shoves her tiny hand in the narrow space in between. She grins.

"Bingo." She holds up a very small tin box in triumph.

"Oh my God," I yelp before clamping a hand over my mouth. Toby grabs the box. I grab the box from Toby. Izumi jumps up and down. The guard tells us to simmer down or else.

"Open it, open it!"

Our excitement dims considerably when I pry open the box to reveal a miniature videotape. "What is it?" I ask, holding it up for inspection.

"MicroMV," Izumi says immediately. "Only produced for a few years by Sony back in the early 2000s. Obsolete technology."

"How do we see what's on there?" Charlotte asks.

"Do you happen to have a MicroMV camcorder?" Toby asks, rolling his eyes in disgust.

"I don't even know what that is."

"This tape is useless," he says, "unless we can find a camera to play it on."

"We could find an old tourist and bribe him," Charlotte suggests.

"No self-respecting tourist uses this kind of camera anymore," Izumi says. The rush of success is all but gone. "We should go back to school and just give this to Mrs. Smith. Maybe we won't get in trouble because she's been looking for it?"

"Are you crazy?" Charlotte snaps. "There has to be one of these cameras somewhere in this city, and I'm not going anywhere until I see what's on that tape. Wasn't that the whole point of this anyway?"

"I'm with Charlotte on this one," Izumi says. "I want to see what everyone has gone so insane over."

"But where do we find a camera?" I ask. "Realistically, I mean, because I don't think the tourist angle is going to work."

Toby looks uncomfortable. He's also suspiciously quiet. "What?" I demand.

"Nothing," he says.

"You're lying," I say. "No lying on this quest."

"Don't call it a quest," he says. "You sound like a dork."

"You can try and distract me by being all grouchy, but there's something you're not telling us."

Toby looks defeated. "Fine. There may be a way to watch this tape."

"Well, why didn't you say so in the first place?" demands Charlotte.

He glares at her. "Follow me," he tells us. "And try to keep up."

We walk thirteen blocks so quickly my blisters get blisters. When we finally come to a stop, we're all panting.

I stare up at an opulent building. Until I got to Smith, I didn't really associate with superrich people. This place is literally golden.

"Why are we here?" asks Izumi.

"I live here," Toby says glumly.

We gawk. "Like in this building, here?" I ask.

"Well, I never said I liked it." Toby pushes into the lobby and we follow.

The lobby reminds me of a cruise ship with enormous sparkling chandeliers and towering gold fountains. The floors are pink marble and so shiny I can see my reflection. Toby cuts diagonally and heads for an elevator bank. We follow like ducklings. A guy in a uniform wearing a BRAD name tag gives Toby a high five.

"Where you been, Tobias?" Brad asks cheerfully. "It's been months."

"Dad's in Saudi Arabia," Toby replies. "Or Singapore? I forget which. I'm just picking up a few things for school. These are my friends."

"Well, it's nice to meet you, friends of Toby," Brad says with a grin. He hustles us into the elevator, sending us off with a friendly wave. As we race skyward, Toby looks more and more glum. He, too, is the only child of a single parent, and while I know this is sometimes hard, he looks downright depressed at the thought of going home. Of course, a dad like Drexel Caine might do that to you. Lately, the man has taken to posting YouTube videos of his wacky late-night experiments with robots and rockets and weird kitchen appliances. He's sure to show up on reality TV any day now.

"So," I say quietly. "Why did you bring us here?"

"The Collection," Izumi says thoughtfully.

"The Collection!" Charlotte exclaims. "Of course!" Toby looks at his feet.

"Can someone please explain?" I ask.

"The Obsolete Technology Collection," Izumi says, as if I should know this. "The *New York Times* did a whole article on it a few years ago."

Before I can figure out why I should care, the elevator glides to a smooth stop on the top floor of the tower. The penthouse. The elevator doors open directly into an elaborate vestibule, decorated with modern sculpture of naked people. If I laugh, I will demonstrate a total lack of sophistication. I bite my tongue.

Toby presses his thumb to a pad and the front doors swing open. I've been a lot of places, and I've never seen anything like this. It's like putting whipped cream on top of the frosting of a chocolate layer cake. It's almost too much.

Toby remains silent as we pass through a tennis-court-size living room with stunning views to the west. The furniture, straight out of a magazine, doesn't look as if it's ever been used. We walk across a kitchen designed to feed a small invading army. There are bedrooms and sitting rooms and an enormous office with floor-to-ceiling bookshelves. Our footsteps echo in the silence. The whole place feels as unlived-in as the Frick. I can't believe Toby grew up here.

We reach a large steel door at the far end of the apartment. Toby enters a passcode and the door yields. Fluorescent lighting comes on overhead, revealing a space the size of a football field. I know it can't be that big, but it sure looks like it.

"The lab," Izumi whispers. "From the videos."

"Yeah," says Toby.

The lab is freezing and crowded with glass museum-style cases. "Drexel collects obsolete technology," Toby explains. "He has this whole thing about only knowing where we're going if we know where we've been and blah, blah, blah. Anyway, this is where he keeps his junk. Now all we gotta do is find that camcorder from last century, because I know it's here somewhere."

Talk about a needle in a haystack. Drexel may well be

a genius, but he's a very disorganized one. There are piles of old phonographs and turntables and ham radios and ancient-looking telegraph machines. There are cases full of reel-to-reel recorders and VCRs and Betamax machines. And for every item I can identify, there are dozens that might as well be from another planet. According to Toby, Drexel just knows where everything is, which makes for slow going.

After the first hour of searching, Charlotte peels off to raid the giant refrigerator and watch TV. At hour two, Izumi leaves to use the bathroom and never comes back.

By hour three I'm ready to cry and admit defeat, but just as I am, I hear Toby yell, "Yes!" He holds something in the air. "Sony's finest, circa 2000. Now we can watch the tape."

Chapter 31

WHERE WE BATTLE OLD TECHNOLOGY. AND MOSTLY LOSE.

IT TAKES ANOTHER HALF AN HOUR to find the right cables to plug in the camcorder, probably dead since before we were born. Toby yells a lot and rampages around the lab, flinging open drawers and cabinets. I stand in the corner, trying to stay out of his way. Eventually Toby finds the cables under this brick-size hunk of plastic he swears is a cell phone from the 1980s. How would you even carry that thing? You'd need a suitcase! Izumi and Charlotte return. They look well fed and relaxed. I hand Toby the tape. He loads it into the camera and an image appears on the tiny screen. We all huddle in close and squint.

A little girl, probably not even two, is running around

in a diaper. There's a kiddie pool on the lawn and a few other kid toys, and you can tell the little girl is just having the best time throwing herself in the pool. The sound quality is pretty bad, but she's clearly laughing, falling into the water, and getting back up to do it again. Whoever is filming is gesturing for her to do things. The little girl sits in the pool kicking her chubby legs and yelling, "Dada play! Dada play! Dada play!" over and over again. The sound quality is poor, so the girl sounds off, warped somehow.

The shot jerks as the camcorder is dropped on the lawn. When the man retrieves it, we get a full-on look at his face. He seems ordinary. Toby pauses the tape.

"I don't recognize him," he says. "Do you guys?" We all shake our heads and he lets the tape roll.

The girl races at her father and mashes her face right up against the camera.

"Now, be careful, honey," the man says. "We need to take care of that boo-boo." The little girl's hand flies to her face, which fills the screen. Along the left side of her jawline is a tight row of black stitches, stark against her pale skin. My palms grow clammy. I look at Toby, and his eyes are wide.

The girl pulls back as the man runs his fingers down her cheek. "Daddy loves you, sweet pea," he says. His voice cracks, but I can't tell if it's emotion or the poor quality of the tape. "Yes, he does. And Daddy will always love Ronny, no matter what happens. Daddy loves Ronny."

Toby leaps to his feet. "Did that man just say what I think he said?" he asks.

"He said Ronny," I say. "You don't think . . ."

"What are you guys talking about?" says Charlotte.

Toby fumbles with the camera and the video starts at the beginning. We watch the same scenes unfold before us. "It's her," Toby says.

"No way," I say, wanting him to be wrong.

"You don't know her like I do," he says loudly. "You don't watch her every move. You don't have to . . ."

We stare at him. A red glow rises in his cheeks. "Sorry," he mutters. "It's just I know it's her. I know it."

Charlotte stomps her foot. "What are you talking about?"

"Veronica!" we shout in unison.

"Wait," says Izumi. "*The* Veronica? As in Veronica Brooks, who was dead and came back to life and is terrifying? That Veronica?"

"Yes!"

"You think that's her on the tape?" Izumi sounds incredulous. I don't blame her.

"The scar," Toby says. "He calls her Ronny. Plus I just know it's her."

"Because you stalk her, right?" says Charlotte. Toby looks ready to pounce.

"Okay, okay, okay," I say, holding up my hands for us to all just slow down. "If that kid really is Veronica and this is the evidence Jennifer found against the Ghost, does that mean . . ."

"His weakness," Toby says. "The one Teflon was searching for."

"But I've seen her parents on campus," Izumi says. "And that guy isn't her dad."

"Veronica's adopted," Charlotte throws out. "Did you guys know that? Her family has a house on the Vineyard near ours, and I remember overhearing her mom telling my mom how lucky they were to have her and what a great kid she was and all that."

In stunned silence, we stare at the image of a small Veronica on the video screen. For the first time since this started, I have the distinct feeling I'm in way over my head.

"This is so not good," Toby whispers. "You guys don't understand what the Ghost does. He gets rid of people, anyone who gets in his way, anyone who knows something he shouldn't. One day you just wake up and discover you've vanished. And honestly, I don't think he'll be pleased knowing that we know what we know. This is too big. It's way bigger than us. We're screwed." He runs his fingers through his hair.

"You're totally losing it," I point out.

"And you aren't?" he yelps.

Izumi, Charlotte, and I look at one another. Izumi's eyes are wide, but she's calm. Charlotte fidgets, but she's not unglued. "Nope," I say. "Not like you."

Toby sits down on a pile of old hard drives. He puts his head between his knees like he's in a plane that's about to crash. "I don't feel well," he says.

Seriously? Toby bolts from the lab. I grab the camera and follow. Izumi and Charlotte bring up the rear. Toby races for one of the twenty-seven bathrooms and we wait in the living room. Toby eventually comes back and drapes himself dramatically across the couch. Charlotte examines him critically. "I'd say that graduate spy school thing in Florida is right out," she says.

"Yeah," says Izumi, "you're a mess."

"Is this why you don't go out in the field?" I ask.

"No! I'm too young. So are you. This is not what Lower Middles or Middles are supposed to be doing!" He rests the back of his palm on his forehead.

"What now, Abby?" Izumi asks.

The urge to pace is overwhelming. Fortunately, Toby's living room is a mile long. "I hate to say it, but I think we have to hand the tape over to Mrs. Smith. Toby's right about one thing: This is bigger than us."

"Agreed," says Charlotte. "Do you think the Center will use Veronica to get the Ghost? Like the way they used you to find Jennifer?"

This idea gives me a sick feeling in my stomach. I'm not one of Veronica's adoring minions, but I still hate the idea of her being used like I was. It didn't feel good. "I don't know," I say. Veronica's whole world is the Center. Sure, she excels at practically everything, but I can tell how much the spy gig means to her. Is anyone going to care about her being collateral damage? I shake this off. I've proven my value by finding the tape, and now it's time to step back.

Suddenly, Toby sits bolt upright on the couch. "What's that smell?"

"Huh?"

"Something burning," he says, sniffing the air. "You guys don't smell it?"

"Like plastic maybe?" Charlotte asks.

Toby leaps up. "Oh no!" He darts toward the small table on the other side of the living room where I put the camcorder with the videotape still inside. It's a smoldering pile of goo throwing off tendrils of smoke. Toby grabs a vase full of wilted flowers and dumps the water on the camcorder. It sizzles and pops. What's left behind is a big, disgusting mess.

"That did not just happen," Toby moans. "The find of the century, ruined."

"Really ruined," I say, standing beside him.

He kicks the table with his foot and sends the whole melted muddle flying across the room. "And that's why those camcorders don't exist today!" he yells. "They stink! The worst!"

"We can still tell Mrs. Smith what we saw," I say. "It's not a complete disaster."

Toby gets right up in my face. "This would have been enough to get me into the strategy school. This would have been enough to write my own ticket. But now we have nothing. Nothing!"

"Maybe the tape was meant to do that?" Izumi interrupts.

This stops Toby's rant in its footsteps. "What do you mean?"

"Like self-destruct. It happens in the movies."

"That's insane."

"I thought a spy school for girls was insane," I point out.

"No way," Toby says. But he walks over and picks up the hunk of plastic, examining it from all angles. And he doesn't put it down when he leaves to call for a car to take us back to Smith.

We spend the half hour waiting for the car in the enormous kitchen, eating gelato imported from Rome and chocolate truffles with actual gold flakes on them or something, which greatly improves our collective mood. When Brad buzzes to tell us the car has arrived, we're in relatively high spirits. There will be consequences (toilet cleaning, tutoring stupid hockey players) for going AWOL from Smith, but we're ready, come what may. As Toby said, we have made the find of the century. Sort of, anyway.

Chapter 32

WHERE I REALIZE THE IMPORTANCE OF LESSON NUMBER ONE.

A GIANT SHINY BLACK embarrassment waits for us at the curb. Brad holds the door as we pile into the Hummer limo.

"Really, Toby?" Izumi says. "This is the car you picked?"

Toby shrugs. "I used my dad's account. This is what he likes." At least the windows are tinted so we can't be seen from the outside. The driver sits behind a smoky glass partition. All we see of him is a faint outline.

"You kids all set?" Brad asks. He reaches in, gives Toby another high five, and off we go. We're quiet, each spinning private scenarios of how things will go down back at Smith. My hope (delusion) is that when we tell Mrs. Smith about the videotape, she'll be so distracted she'll forget about punishing us, at least for a little while.

Clearly, everyone is lost in their own thoughts, because we've been driving a good twenty minutes before Izumi realizes we're not headed north toward Connecticut but have veered east toward Queens. Izumi grips my thigh.

"Look out the window," she whispers. I do but see only the gray blur of New York City in winter.

"Yeah?"

"Queens," she hisses. It takes me a moment to register. Queens? Oh no. Queens! I lean forward and whisper this news to Toby, who passes it along to Charlotte, a life-and-death game of telephone.

"Maybe it's a shortcut?" Charlotte says quietly.

"Um, no," Toby says. "It's the wrong direction entirely."

"I really don't want to do this," I mutter. I crawl on my knees toward the partition separating us from the driver and rap on the glass gently with my knuckles. This close-up, I can see the man is dressed in a black suit and wears a cap.

"Excuse me?" I say. "We're headed to Watertown, Connecticut? To the Smith School?"

The driver tightens his grip on the wheel but otherwise doesn't appear to have heard me. Maybe the glass is sound-proof. I knock harder. The driver twitches. I think I'm coming in loud and clear, but maybe he doesn't speak English?

"Watertown, Connecticut?" I say slowly, overemphasizing each syllable.

The driver pushes a button and the partition slides down. And then the driver rotates toward me. And then I wish that she hadn't. The man in the suit and cap is none other than my old pal Fake Bronwyn.

"You!" I shout. "You drowned in that lake!" My friends jump.

"I'm tougher than any little frozen puddle, Abigail," she says with a nasty grin.

"You know this person?" Charlotte asks.

"Yes! And she's not nice!"

"Oh, come on," Fake Bronwyn protests. "I'm plenty nice. It's just that you aren't paying me. Please pass your backpacks into the front seat."

Instead, I lunge across Toby for the door. So what that we're traveling at sixty miles an hour in traffic? But of course it's locked and there is no obvious way to unlock it from back here. I should have seen that right away! When will I learn?

"Good try," Fake Bronwyn says, grinning again. "Backpacks, please."

"Hey," I say. "I tried to help you in that lake!"

"Probably the wrong choice, in hindsight."

"You saved her?" Charlotte asks, indignant.

I shrug. "A little." I don't bother explaining that I'd thought by letting her drown I'd be as bad as the bad guys. In light of current circumstances, that thinking is flawed.

"Where are you taking us?" Toby demands.

"The boy wonder." Fake Bronwyn smirks.

"Is your real name Suzie?" I interrupt.

"Huh?"

"Tom called you Suzie," I say. "Is that your name?"

"I have lots of names," she says.

"Where are we going?" Toby asks again.

"Queens," Bronwyn says. "JFK."

The airport? This is bad. This is very bad. They're going to whisk us away to a horrible prison in Bulgaria, never to be heard from again.

Just as I am about to lose it, I remember all is not lost! In my jacket is the fancy pink leopard-print iPhone, turned off as Toby insisted. The hot water is gone, but I still have the rubber bullet and the whistle. I work through the problem. If I pull out the phone and shoot Bronwyn with the rubber bullet, she'll probably crash the car. If I do the whistle, it will incapacitate us all, and she'll probably crash the car. And I'm not certain we can escape from this car. So maybe I wait until we stop and get out? But then what if they discover I have the iPhone? Or handcuff us or something? This on-the-fly spy scheming is difficult work. I decide to wait. I place my hand in my pocket and nudge Toby, revealing just the edge of the phone case. He grins.

Fifteen minutes later we roll into a hangar on the outskirts of the enormous John F. Kennedy Airport. We drive straight past a small passenger jet to the back of the hangar, where the entire Hummer limo pulls into a freight elevator. The doors slide shut and we begin a quick descent. I start to regret not using the whistle or the bullet and taking our chances in the daylight. We will meet our end like the rats living under the city.

"I don't like this," Charlotte says quietly.

"Me either," I say. Finally, we stop. The elevator opens to reveal a dimly lit concrete basement. A tomb, and that's being kind. Several dark tunnels lead away in different directions. The car doors unlock with a click. We climb out, greeted by two armed men dressed in commando black, who apparently don't like kids because they don't smile or say hello. Instead, one zip-ties our hands behind our backs while the other looks menacing. Fake Bronwyn sets off down one of the tunnels, and the guards shove us after her. One of them scoops up our backpacks. I seriously miscalculated. Now our hands are tied. Literally.

"Let's have a chat, shall we?" Fake Bronwyn says, tossing her black cap aside.

We continue down the hallway, passing three closed doors until stopping in front of a fourth. A guard steps forward and unlocks the door while the other stands to Toby's left, distracted by his cuticles. It's enough. I take advantage of this micro-opportunity to turn the phone on and tuck it in the back of my pants, where it will be less obvious. This is no easy thing with my zip-tied hands, but I manage without giving myself away. The phone is so pleased to be back in business it gives out a digital yelp of delight. I cough violently to cover the sound, but Fake Bronwyn wheels around.

"What was that?" she demands.

"What was what?" I ask innocently.

"There was a noise," she says. The guards shrug, noncommittal. They just lock and unlock doors and look threatening. They have no opinion otherwise.

"I didn't hear anything," Toby says.

Fake Bronwyn pokes him in the sternum. "You be quiet," she says.

The door swings in to reveal a classic interrogation room, right out of the *Law & Order* reruns we can't get enough of at McKinsey House. The guards push us inside, into four metal seats opposite a sturdy metal table. Fake Bronwyn sits at the table and daintily crosses her legs. I notice she has big feet for her size. Our backs face the wall, which gives me an opportunity to slide the iPhone up under my too-tight tank top using the inner edge of my elbow. If I don't sweat too much, it should stay mostly in place and out of view.

The guard with the mustache rolls a tray into the room. It contains a hammer, a screwdriver, a small saw, and a few shiny silver implements straight from the dentist's office. I avert my eyes because staring at the tray makes me sweat, and the more I sweat the more likely it is the iPhone will slide down my back and onto the floor. The guards retreat to the corners, where they stand stock-still like they're auditioning for the Queen's Guard. Fake Bronwyn opens our backpacks and dumps the contents out on the table. Our belongings scatter right to the edges. My hairbrush and Chinese History book. A scarf and pair of gloves. Three tubes of ChapStick. Eyeliner. Eyeliner? Where did Charlotte think we were going, anyway? There's my Smith School water bottle and a bunch of cables that must belong to Toby. Granola bars. A can of Coke. The pencil sketch of Persephone. The melted hunk of camcorder.

Fake Bronwyn picks through the pile, examining our

stuff, breezing right over the camcorder. She picks up a battery similar to the one Toby gave me before I went to California.

"What's this?" she asks, shoving it up under Toby's nose.

"It's a battery. For a phone." Fake Bronwyn raises an eyebrow, takes the hammer off the tray, and smashes the rectangle. But the hammer bounces off the battery, so she does it again and again and the thing just jumps furiously around the table. Frustrated, she turns the hammer on Toby's iPhone. Bits of plastic and glass fly everywhere. Toby gasps. Fake Bronwyn grins. She smashes the Coke can, which explodes, and the eyeliner, which turns to mush. In a frenzy now, she even gives the Chinese History book a whack. Charlotte winces with each blow. Izumi squeezes her eyes shut and makes a very unpleasant face. I'm sure they're regretting coming along with me, because I'm certainly regretting bringing them. I concentrate on the leopard-print iPhone slowly sliding down my back. I can't stop sweating. In a minute, our last chance at survival will slip to the floor.

Satisfied she's destroyed everything that needs destroying, Bronwyn sweeps the debris aside with her arm and leans over the table, right in my face. "Tell me where it is," she says. "Or else."

Chapter 33

WHERE THINGS GET LOUD.

IF I LIVE, I SWEAR I'LL REFORM. I'll watch *Charlie's Angels* reruns without rolling my eyes. I'll go back to calling Jennifer "Mom." I'll make my bed. Clean my room. Get straight As. I'll never make another sassy remark again, ever, about anything. Well, at least I'll try really hard not to. There are things I want to do in life! I want to master a backflip off the high dive and climb Mount Everest. I'm not prepared to have everything come to an end in this room.

"Where is it?" Fake Bronwyn asks again.

"Where's what?" I try very hard not to cast my eyes in the direction of the melted camcorder now on the floor.

Fake Bronwyn gets up and circles behind us. I don't

like her behind me. If she spots the iPhone shoved up my shirt, we're in trouble. Not that we aren't already. She picks a razor off the tray and passes it under my nose. "I'm really sick of you making me look bad," she whispers.

The phone drops another centimeter. I wiggle in my seat. "I don't know what you're talking about."

"The videotape!" She smashes the table with both fists. I jump. Izumi's still making that awful face, but now I realize she's been working the zip-tie handcuffs the whole time. And she's got her hands free! Without missing a beat, Izumi leaps from her chair and hits Fake Bronwyn in the ribs with her shoulder. Classic rugby move. Fake Bronwyn goes flying and hits the far wall hard. She comes down in a heap.

There's a lot of screaming. Izumi spins gracefully and launches a metal chair at one of the guards, nailing him right in the head. He goes down too.

"That's enough of that!" shrieks the second guard. "Nobody move!" He waves his gun around at us and we freeze. And this is the moment the iPhone slides from my shirt. I manage to catch it in my bound hands just before it falls. "Toby is cool!" I yell. "Whistle!"

To describe the sound emanating from the phone as "deafening" doesn't quite do it justice. Deafening would be a pleasure. Mix a howling cat with nails on a chalkboard. Throw in a side of screaming baby and a dash of the 4 train screeching into Astor Place station. Now turn it up loud, real loud, loud enough to shatter glass, and maybe you're halfway to understanding what we have going on.

The guard drops his gun and falls to his knees, hands over ears. I can't tell if he screams, but his mouth is open. I think I might vomit. The noise is so loud I see stars. Charlotte doubles over. Toby turns a funny color. I fight through the stars.

Squinting helps.

Izumi grabs Toby's Swiss Army Knife off the ground, throws open the door, and herds us out. The stars multiply in my head, a virtual milky way of noise-induced hallucinations.

Wait! Toby mouths. He snatches the unbreakable plastic rectangle, along with the screaming iPhone.

"What are you doing?" I yell.

"I haven't gotten the patents on this yet! I can't just leave it here!"

Our lives are on the line, and Toby's worried about intellectual property? Izumi gives us a final shove and we lurch out of the room. She throws the lock on the door behind us.

"Tell it to shut off, Abby!" Toby yells. *How is it ever going to hear me?*

"Toby is cool!" I howl. "iPhone off!" Instant silence.

"Cut us loose," I say to Izumi. Or I think I say that. I can't actually hear my own voice. Quickly, Izumi frees us from the plastic handcuffs, and we stumble down the tunnel, careening off the walls like drunk people.

"I. Am. A. Genius," Toby declares. "I feel really bad right now, but that was brilliant, right? The noise thing? Totally incapacitating!"

Once Jennifer brought me to a Rolling Stones concert. The guys were like fossils and I didn't like the music and by the end of the show, I felt like my head was stuffed with cotton. This is much, much worse. It's a noise concussion.

"Save your self-congratulations for daylight," I mumble. Our equilibrium is off, and we keep bumping into one another.

"Why did you keep yelling *Toby is cool*?" Charlotte asks, wiggling her jaw around as if to pop her ears.

"Ask him," I say, gesturing in the general direction of Toby. I am not sure which way is which at the moment.

"Maybe later," she says. Toby has both fingers jammed in his ears and is making a weird face.

Finally, we stagger into the room where the Hummer is parked.

"I think I'm ready to go home now," Izumi says quietly.

I can't agree more. "Let's get out of here," I say. But maybe not as fast as all that. Two new guards appear from the dark tunnel, armed and ready.

"Freeze!" one of them yells. "Hands up!" This makes me giggle. It's stress, but I can't help it. *Hands up* is way too cliché.

"Stop laughing!" says Izumi, elbowing me hard.

"I don't know if I can," I say, laughing.

"You," one of the guards shouts, "quit doing that."

"I can't," I say. Meanwhile, Toby waves his arms in the air like he's under attack by a swarm of bees. This makes me laugh harder. I'm totally losing it.

"Freeze and don't move," the guard says. "Put your arms down. Stop talking. Stop laughing!"

"But you just said *Hands up*," I say.

"Listen, kid," he snarls. "Don't think I won't shoot you, 'cause I will."

"I totally believe you," Toby says. I realize while flailing, he's managed to remove the battery from his pocket.

"Hey, what's that?" a guard asks, coming closer. "Put that down!"

"Get behind me!" Toby yells. We leap back. He aims the

rectangle at the charging guards and presses a button not visible to the untrained eye. The device explodes with such force Toby is thrown back into us. We hit the wall hard and land in a twisted heap, but the guards are stopped dead in their tracks, completely covered in sticky yellow webbing. The more they struggle, the more entangled they become.

"I call it Black Widow," Toby says from the floor.

"Nice," Izumi says.

The guards curse a blue streak. They call us names Jennifer would ground me for in a heartbeat. As we untangle and stand, I hear a sickening crunch.

"What was that?" asks Charlotte.

"Oh my God, Abby!" Izumi screams. "Was that your leg?"

I glance down at my leg. It looks normal, no blood or bones sticking out, but I move and again the crunch. It's the iPhone. Or what's left of it. My fancy spy iPhone is toast, its screen black, the glass shattered. I hold it in my hands like an injured baby bird. The high-velocity rubber bullet falls to the floor. I never even got to use it.

"Aw, man," says Toby, crestfallen.

"I'm sorry," I stammer. "I must have fallen on it weird. . . ."

"Don't worry about it," he says. "I can make another. I think I can, anyway."

The guard calls me a particularly rude name and I'm not feeling all that forgiving on account of a few moments ago he threatened to shoot us. I stuff the crushed phone in my back pocket, march right up to him, and—BAM—hit him right between the eyes with the heel of my hand.

"That's called the *Shut up* maneuver," I say. Izumi and Charlotte burst out laughing. We've gone off the deep end.

"The elevator!" I yell. And we run.

Chapter 34

WHERE WE'RE OUT OF THE WOODS. BUT ONLY FOR A MINUTE.

WE'RE GIDDY WITH OUR OWN awesomeness by the time we reach the elevator. We just escaped the clutches of Fake Bronwyn, evil henchwoman to the Ghost.

But I remember Jennifer telling me that climbing to the top of Mount Everest was no big deal. The hard part was getting back down. True, we're out of the dungeon, but we haven't actually gotten away yet.

This sinks in as the elevator slowly ascends and we each contemplate the individual horrors that might await us at the top. The phone is dead. We've used the Black Widow. We have nothing left but our wits.

"I wish I had the Spy Eye right now," Toby says.

"Why?" I ask. "So you could plaster the elevator with terrifying images of Veronica?"

"You aren't still mad about that, are you?"

"I might be."

"Why is this elevator taking so long?" Charlotte groans. "We've been in here for days!"

"Spy Eye could see if they're waiting for us at the top," Toby says. "Not that we can do very much about it. But still. I can't believe you fainted that night in Mrs. Smith's office."

Izumi and Charlotte giggle despite our precarious circumstances. "You totally did," says Charlotte.

"Is now really when you want to have this conversation?" I ask.

"You fainted dead away in front of Mrs. Smith and Mr. Roberts." Toby snickers.

You know that moment when you've been playing Minecraft on hard mode and the hostile mobs are spawning, the creepers swarm and zombies are busting through the doors? You're sure you're dead, but suddenly you make it through and level up. The whole thing clicks into place and makes sense. I have that moment now. Except not with a video game.

"Mr. Roberts was in the office that night too?" I ask, confused. "Beginning Concepts in Physics Mr. Roberts?"

"Yeah," Toby says. But before I can say another word, the elevator grinds to a halt and the door slides open. And standing there is not a band of armed guards ready to drag us back to the dungeon but Mr. Roberts himself.

Izumi and Charlotte run to him. "Oh my God," wails Charlotte. "I really thought we were going to die down there. How did you find us? Can we please leave? I'm so happy to see you!"

"You kids are in a heap of trouble," Mr. Roberts says with a friendly wink. "Mrs. Smith sent me to escort you home, but traffic was terrible and I almost didn't make it."

"We need to get out of here!" Toby says, breathless. "It's the Ghost! Or we think it is. Anyway, we found the evidence on him and, well, it burned up, but we saw it before that happened."

Mr. Roberts holds up a hand for us to calm down and be quiet. "Did you say you found the tape but it burned up?"

"Wait," I say. I remember the night in the office, way back when this crazy ride began. If the man in the chair was Mr. Roberts, then it was Mr. Roberts who was desperate to get the evidence. It was Mr. Roberts who pushed Mrs. Smith to use me. And that was no bruise on his leg. It was a triangle tattoo, pledging allegiance to the very bad guy he was supposed to be hunting.

Mr. Roberts is the traitor.

"Oh no," I murmur.

But Toby, so eager to please our supposed savior, continues to babble. "We played the tape on one of those old camcorders a few times and we think we know why the Ghost wanted it back so badly."

"Toby, shut up," I whisper, elbowing him.

"You think you know, do you?" asks Mr. Roberts.

"It's Veronica!" Izumi yelps. "On the tape."

"We think the Ghost is her dad," adds Charlotte.

"We could use this against him, right?" says Toby.

"You say the tape burned up?" Mr. Roberts asks again.

"You guys," I say. "Mrs. Smith didn't send him." But they don't hear me.

"The tape is actually down there with those people who kidnapped us," Toby says. "But it's useless, just a hunk of messed-up plastic."

"But you watched it before that happened?"

"Yes."

"All of you?"

"Yes. A few times," says Izumi. "We have the details down, I swear."

"I bet you do," Mr. Roberts says with a smirk. "You didn't by any chance have the opportunity to copy it, did you?"

Toby hangs his head. "No," he whispers. "We should have. That was a mistake. I'll be more thorough next time."

"On the contrary," Mr. Roberts says. "That's just fine in this situation. Now, why don't we all just hop in the car and take a little ride?"

"No!" I shout. My friends look at me as if I've lost my mind. "He's one of them."

"Abby, what are you saying?" Izumi asks.

Mr. Roberts smiles benignly. "You've had a long couple of days, Abigail. You're just confused. Tired."

Behind Roberts, I see the guards, three of them in the shadows. They're armed and dressed in black and look an awful lot like the guys we just left downstairs tangled up in all the yellow goo. But they don't run at us or yell or wave those guns around as you would if your prey was escaping. They're waiting patiently for orders.

"Abby," Charlotte hisses. "What are you doing?"

"He's going to take us to the Ghost," I say, my mouth dry. "Because we saw the tape."

"What?" Toby says. "Why?"

"Because he works for him!" I scream. This finally gets their attention. They look from me to Mr. Roberts and back to me.

"She's talking nonsense," Mr. Roberts says. "She's stressed and scared and desperate not to look like a fool. Are you actually going to listen to her?"

"He has a triangle tattoo," I blurt. "On his ankle. I saw it. He works for the Ghost. You have to believe me." The guards move silently forward.

And my friends fall into line beside me. "We believe Abby," says Izumi.

Mr. Roberts's face twists into something ugly. His eyes blaze, and his lips form a thin tight line. His lips curl in a nasty smile, and when he speaks, his voice is much deeper than it was mere moments ago.

"Abigail Hunter," he says with a sneer. "Look what the little missy thinks she's figured out. Just like your mother, constantly messing with things that have nothing to do with you." He takes me by the shoulders and shakes me ever-so-slightly. "You've caused a lot of problems."

"So I guess that's something I can be proud of," I say. He slaps me. My friends gasp. A small trickle of blood runs from my nose. My cheek stings and my eyes threaten to overflow, but I won't cry, not in front of this man. I refuse to give him the satisfaction.

"Did you copy the tape?" he demands.

"No," I say. "We already said we didn't."

"We have ways of finding out for sure," he says, shoving me toward the car.

I can see daylight out the wide hangar entrance. A black car pulls up close to the building and someone climbs out. The guards circle up as if to contain us.

A lone person wearing dark clothes and a baseball cap strides into the hangar. My imagination runs wild. Is this the guy whose specialty is torturing innocent kids? Or does Roberts do his own dirty work? Maybe this newcomer is a guard late for work? But no. This person is none of these.

First, the guards fall unconscious to the ground (*Thunk! Thunk! Thunk!*). Tiny colorful darts are just barely visible in their necks. Before Roberts registers any of this, the person in the cap holds a gun to the back of his head.

"Don't move," my mother says. "Don't even think about it."

Chapter 35

WHERE WE PLAY A GAME.

I HAVE NEVER BEEN SO GLAD to see Jennifer Hunter in all my life, including that time I got lost in Central Park when I was six. "Mom!" I yell.

"Hello, kids," she says with a wave.

"Oh, Mrs. Hunter!" Izumi says. "It's really good to meet you!" Toby stares at Jennifer as if she's Superman or Spider-Man or some awesome hybrid of the two.

"It's good to meet you all too," she says. "I'm sorry I missed you guys at the museum, but some of Roberts's goons tripped me up for a bit. Almost worked, too. I'm kind of rusty."

"You're something much worse than rusty," Roberts growls. Jennifer pushes the barrel of the gun in an inch.

"You were right under our noses the whole time," she says, shaking her head. "The Center forces you into retirement and you join the bad guys. I have to say I never saw it coming."

"I gave my life to the Center," he cries. "And they kick me out for Lola Smith. They retire me into teaching the little brats."

"You betrayed your friends, your country, everything. You went to work for the Ghost," Jennifer replies.

"And how is what I did any worse than what you did? Everything I did for you, all those years of training, of work, and you throw it away for her." Roberts glares at me.

For the first time, my mother looks angry. "You twisted old man," she says quietly. "I'm nothing like you. Abby, come over here. There's a zip tie in my pocket. Tie his hands behind his back. Now."

I pull the zip tie from Jennifer's pocket. Roberts puts his hands behind his back. I drop the zip tie on the ground. When I bend to retrieve it, Roberts shoves Jennifer with his hands and grabs me, one arm tight around my neck. There's screaming, but I can't tell from who. I claw at his arm with my hands.

"Put down the gun," Roberts commands.

"This isn't about her," Jennifer says.

"Do it now!" Jennifer lays the gun at her feet and kicks it toward him. "Hands in the air. If I see you so much as twitch, I squeeze. And you know I will." Jennifer winces but keeps her hands steady. "Now," Roberts says. "We're going to get in the elevator and take a little trip downstairs, got it?"

"Okay," Jennifer says. "Understood."

As Roberts tries to walk with me held in front of him, I hear the beep. It's a quiet sound, small and a little desperate but definitely there. There's even a vibration in my pocket. The smashed iPhone lives! And I have an idea.

"Do you like card games?" I gasp.

"What?" Roberts asks.

"Abby, no!" yells Toby.

But it's too late. "Toby is cool!" I scream. "Solitaire!"

And that's the last thing I remember.

Chapter 36

ANOTHER TURN FOR THE WEIRD. AND PROBABLY NOT THE LAST ONE.

I'M RIGHT BACK WHERE I STARTED. Nurse Willow holds my hand and tells me it's time to wake up. My whole body aches, as if I've been run over by a bus. "You're just fine, dear," she says. "Or you will be soon. Now, don't sit up too fast."

Of course I do, and the world spins in lazy disorienting circles. I flop back on my pillow.

"I think she's faking it," I hear someone say. Izumi.

"It's been days." I open my eyes and see Toby peering down at me. He has a bandage on his arm. Izumi wears a patch over one eye. Charlotte's hair looks singed. And there's Veronica, standing with her arms across her chest, somehow managing to look happy and annoyed at the same time. But she's here.

"What happened?" I whisper, but my voice is raw and the effort stings.

"We played a card game," Toby says with a smile. "Roberts lost."

"They got him?" I ask.

My friends nod. "All locked up," says Charlotte.

I gasp. "Izumi, your eye?"

"Temporary," she says with a shrug. "Although I might keep the patch. Like embracing my inner pirate, you know?"

I start to cry. I can't say why. I'm grateful to be alive. I'm grateful my friends are alive. I'm glad we caught a bad guy. Jennifer appears in the doorway.

"There's my girl," she says. We hug. My friends and Nurse Willow fade out of the room. After a minute of hugging, I realize I'm being stabbed in the chest by a key she wears around her neck. I push my mother away and take her in. She does not look like Jennifer. She wears a khaki-colored suit. She wears heels. And she wears a key around her neck.

Mrs. Smith's key.

"What's going on?" I gulp.

She runs her fingers down my cheek. "You were very brave," she says. "I'm incredibly proud of you. You're also grounded forever."

"Where were you? Why didn't you save me? Lotus Man, Fake Bronwyn, Evil Tom, Rip Curl!"

Jennifer chuckles. "And here I thought you were going to be upset finding out about the Center and me."

"I am!" I shout.

"Shhh," she whispers. "Calm down, otherwise Nurse Willow will throw me out. I didn't come for you because I didn't know you were in California. I was deep under. The way the partnership worked for so many years was I'd disappear and Lola, I mean Mrs. Smith, would step in and take over. Except that didn't happen. I didn't get a line on you until Charlotte used Uber, at which point I figured out what you were up to. But I ran into some problems with Roberts's men, which slowed me down. All in all, not my best work."

She smiles sadly. "I planned to tell you everything when you were older. I wanted you to make up your own mind about things. My choices don't have to be your choices. But Mrs. Smith should never have dragged you into this. She violated just about every rule in the book."

"Why did she?"

"She was desperate for a win. Desperation can make people do things."

"Are you going to get the Ghost?" I ask quietly. I don't want them to use Veronica. I want them to be better than that.

"Yes," she says. "We'll get him. I've always believed that. But we aren't going to sacrifice your friend to do it."

"Oh, she's not my friend," I say quickly. "She can't stand me."

"I don't know about that," my mother says, smiling. "What I do know is your parents aren't your destiny. You should never have to pay for their mistakes. Every one of you is your own person. Veronica doesn't know what you all saw on the videotape and doesn't need to. She's one of us."

I hug her again so hard I think she gasps. And again, the key stabs me. "What's with the suit?" I ask.

"Well, funny you should ask," she says. I don't like the sound of that. "Mrs. Smith is on a small . . . vacation. And the Center asked me to step in for the time being."

"Wait a minute," I say slowly. "You're the new headmaster?"

"Interim headmaster," she corrects. "To be honest, I'm not sure I can stand these shoes for very long." I'm speechless.

My mother pats my hand. "Now, you just concentrate on getting better," she says, "because we have work to do.

Just between me and you, I've heard rumors about someone named Tucker Harrington that are giving me pause, and I might need your help." She arches an eyebrow and smiles. And I realize she's having fun. The world might be complicated and messy and somewhere out there is the Ghost, but that doesn't matter. Jennifer Hunter has it all under control. More or less, anyway. My mother plants a kiss on my forehead.

"But wait," I croak. "I have more questions! I—"

"I know you do," she interrupts, smoothing my hair. "And I promise I'll answer every one, but now it's time to rest." She kisses me again and she's gone.

It's only after she leaves I notice I'm holding a small piece of paper. It's a pencil sketch of the Persephone Club, the same one from the photograph Toby showed me of the Center's founding class of spies. But the only members of this Persephone Club are Izumi, Charlotte, Toby, and me. We have our arms around each other. I stare at the picture until my eyes flutter with exhaustion. There's still so much I don't understand. So many questions. And so many possible adventures to be had.

Yes. So many adventures.

Acknowledgments

Writing a book is about the most fun I can imagine having. But it's not something I do alone. Nothing happens without the wisdom of my agent, Leigh Feldman, of Leigh Feldman Literary. I'm pretty sure she knows everything. Also, a big shout-out to my editor, Alyson Heller, at Aladdin for taking Abby and her friends and making them shine. The team at Simon & Schuster is top notch, and I'm ever grateful.

I wrote this book for Max and Katie, who inspire me every day with their wit and laughter and spirit. May the world provide you with all the adventures you desire, big and small and amazing. And, finally, this is for Mike, as they all are.

About the Author

BETH McMULLEN is the author of the Mrs. Smith's Spy School for Girls series and several adult mysteries. Her books have heroes and bad guys, action, and messy situations.

An avid reader, she once missed her subway stop and rode the train all the way to Brooklyn because the book she was reading was that good.

She lives in Northern California with her family; two cats; and a parakeet named Zeus, who is sick of the cats eyeballing him like he's dinner.

Visit her at www.BethMcMullenBooks.com.